GU00835871

18 eighteen

a NOVEL

based on a TRUE STORY

J.A. HUSS

eighteen

N^a OVEL

based on a TRUE STORY

18 eighteen
a NOVEL
based on a TRUE STORY
HaUSS

Copyright © 2015 by JA Huss
ISBN: 978-1-944475-82-6

No part of this book may be reproduced in any form or by any electronic or mechanical means, including information storage and retrieval systems, without written permission from the author, except for the use of brief quotations in a book review.

This is a work of fiction. Names, characters, businesses, places, events and incidents are either the products of the author's imagination or used in a fictitious manner. Any resemblance to actual persons, living or dead, or actual events is purely coincidental.

Edited by RJ Locksley
Cover Design by JA Huss

Dedication

For Geoff. My Sunday.
Because you were the best thing about my 18th birthday.

If anger could kill, everyone in this room would be dead. "What do you mean I'm not going to graduate?" I cannot be hearing him correctly.

"I'm sorry, Miss Drake, but you're short."

"I'm not short," I snap. "You just showed me my transcript and I have seven credits more than required for graduation."

"And I just explained to you," Mr. Bowman says with forced patience. "You took your last math class"—he looks down at my schedule and his finger traces the line over to the class name—"AP Geometry, in tenth grade."

"So?"

"So here at Anaheim High School we require you to take one math credit in ninth grade." He looks at my schedule again. "And you did. You took AP Algebra. And then you needed to take another math credit as an upperclassman. You took both your math credits as a lowerclassman."

"But I took them *both*. That's the important part here. I took both."

"I'm afraid these are the rules, Shannon. There's nothing I can do."

"Well, that's fucking stupid." I blurt it out without thinking and I wait for Mr. Bowman to get angry and write me a detention. But he just pinches the bridge of his nose and sighs.

This makes me brave. "It's stupid," I repeat. "You're punishing me for getting my math credits completed early."

"Well, they might make an exception, except that you spent the first half of your junior year in this…" He looks down at my transcript again. "Alternative school."

"I was taking graphic web design. It wasn't some loser school."

"You didn't take math."

"I was done with math!"

"You didn't take science either. That's another problem."

"I took AP Biology."

"In tenth grade. Not eleventh."

"What the fuck is wrong with you people?"

Another guidance counselor looks over at me and scowls. Boy, these Anaheim people must be used to the f-word. Back in Ohio, I'd be expelled if I talked to a counselor like this. But back in Ohio I was ahead in credits too.

"So you need to make up PE."

"I knew that part. You told me that last month. And I have a note from a doctor explaining that my knee was injured last year and it's still very painful, so I have to sit PE out."

"You need to make up driver's ed."

He ignores my note excuse. I don't really mind driver's ed. I don't have my license yet and it's already on my schedule, just like PE.

"You need to make up one semester of science and you can take the other one this semester. And you need to make up one full year of math. We don't have room for you in AP Trig. We don't even have room for you in regular trig this semester. All the trig classes were cancelled since no one passed the first semester."

What kind of school has no trig class? But more importantly... "AP Trig? Are you on drugs? I'm not taking AP Trig. Do you see that D there?" I tap my finger on my schedule over the grade I got for AP Geometry. "I only passed that class because my teacher paid a mafia guy to kill his wife while he was out to dinner with the chief of police and was distracted with attempted murder charges. He said if I got an A on the final, he'd pass me with a D."

Mr. Bowman smiles at me and takes his glasses off. "So you got an A?"

"I did."

"And stop making up stories like that, Shannon. It makes you look crazy."

"That story was true, asshole. When you're living a life like mine, there's no need for lies."

He sighs. Loudly, like he's just about done with me. "The important part of your statement was that your teacher challenged you and you rose to the occasion. I'm confident you will rise to the occasion again."

Defeat washes over me. Dear God. Can this life suck any worse than it already does?

Why, yes, God says. *Yes, it can. You cannot graduate high school, Shannon. Even though you're seven credits ahead.*

I'd get angry, except I'm already angry. I'd yell and scream, but I'm already doing that too. I'd walk out, but what the fuck? I did the work, goddammit. I did the fucking work. How can they punish me for getting it done early?

"Are we in agreement then?" Bowman asks. "You'll do the extra work?"

I look down at my feet for a few seconds before going for pity. "I don't want to rise to the occasion, Mr. Bowman. I want to skate through this last semester the way I've skated through all the ones that came." I look up and meet his eyes. "I don't want to think very hard about anything, I just want to exist right now. And there's no way I can skate through AP Trig. I'm not even *good* at math. They put me in AP Algebra in ninth grade by mistake. I swear to God. And then they refused to let me drop down to a lower class. They forced me to take those AP classes. I can't do trig, Mr. Bowman. I'm not even kidding."

He sighs again. "Look, I should've told you all this when you transferred here last month. But it was two weeks before Christmas vacation and I figured it was best to break the bad news after the holidays. You've been through a lot, Shannon. You've been to five different high schools, three in your junior year alone. So I understand that you're upset and life is difficult right now. But it's not the best time to give up. It's the best time to work harder."

"Upset? Upset doesn't even begin to cover it. You told me I was ahead last semester. I had so many free periods, I was working in the office and the library just to fill out my schedule."

"Again," he says with his practiced sympathetic tone, "I'm sorry. We didn't know what to do with you. Your school in San Diego had you working in the office and library, so we just did what they did."

"Because at that school, I was *ahead*. And it was a helluva lot nicer than this dump."

"And now at this dump, you're behind. I've talked to everyone I could. Now, I can make one more plea before we finalize this, but I'm warning you now, the administration will not give in."

I sigh. I might cry, that's how frustrated I am.

"Would you like me to ask one more time?"

I nod, swallowing down my tears.

"OK. Stay put. Calm down. And I'll be back."

This is not an office, per se. It's a room filled with desks and counselors. Like half a dozen of them. And there are kids everywhere. I suddenly realize lots of people are staring at me, watching me have a meltdown.

My whole face heats up as I glance at the guy next to me. He's built like a quarterback and if he wasn't wearing a black Taking Back Sunday concert shirt, I'd have pegged him as one. But the shirt is a dead giveaway. In high school you are what you wear. "Nice shirt," he says, pointing to my white one that says Cage the Elephant. "You ever see them in concert?"

"Where the fuck do you think I got the shirt?" I snap.

He puts his hands up and smiles. I look away real fast, afraid that he will realize I'm about to start sobbing. I get by in school by being tough. Not mean, just tough. No one can hurt me. But crying in the counseling office does not scream tough. And snapping at a cute guy who was just trying to be nice screams bitch.

Despite my best efforts, my eyes begin to water and my nose starts to run. I start sniffling like crazy.

A thick folder thumps down on Mr. Bowman's desk in front of me and I look up, startled. I stare into the most brilliant green eyes, the most handsome face. He's got a two-day-old beard and I concentrate on his lips as he talks. "Can you let Bowman know that's from me?"

I nod yes, like an idiot. He shoots me a grin and my eyes travel down to his leather jacket and then his hands, where tattoos peek out from under his sleeve. I look back up again, but he just turns away and walks off, his biker boots thudding on the cracked field floors.

What the hell is a guy like that doing in a high school? Probably a narc.

He stops just before turning to leave the outer office and talks to someone. Mr. Bowman peeks his head inside and looks at me.

Then the tattoo guy looks over at me too. What the hell? Definitely a narc.

Mr. Bowman smiles, shakes his hand, and then walks over to me as the biker guy leaves. "OK, well, I did not work a miracle, Shannon. But I did call the alternative school down on Gilbert. That's where you'll need to register for science and math."

Oh, my God. This is really happening. I have to go to night school.

"Your science class is on Tuesday and Thursday afternoons, but you need to get down there today and pre-register. If they don't have enough students before the first day, they cancel the teachers and it's tough getting kids to show up first semester, let alone the second one. We've arranged an exception for your trig class. You are the only student."

"Wonderful."

"I worked very hard to get you that class, Shannon."

I look up at Bowman, feeling a little ashamed. "Sorry. And thank you." But I'm still about to cry over this.

"Now, can you get a ride from your..." He looks down at my folder on his desk. "Brother?"

"Brother-in-law," I correct him.

"Right. Can he take you over to Gilbert for registration after school today?"

I shake my head and look at my shoes.

"Can you ask him?"

I shake my head again.

"Why can't you ask him?"

"He's at work all day and he can't take off for me."

"Can you take the bus?"

"Bus?" Is he kidding? "I come from a small town in Ohio, OK? I took the bus once last year when I lived in San Diego. My best friend and I were trying to go to the mall, but we ended up in Rancho Bernardo. That's a lot of miles in the opposite direction of Fashion Valley Mall, in case you're wondering."

Mr. Bowman laughs. "Well, Gilbert School is straight down Lincoln Avenue. No transfers or anything. Just get on outside the school and get off at Gilbert Street."

I say nothing and just keep looking at my shoes.

"Can you do that, Shannon? Will you go register today?"

"Maybe I don't need to graduate."

"You do. You need to graduate and go to college. You're bright, Shannon. Don't throw your life away because you have a few challenging months ahead of you."

The bell rings so I grab my backpack and stand up, one hundred percent defeated. "Do I at least get to sit out PE?"

"It's this period, and yes. I put you in the modified class. They meet out at the picnic tables next to the bleachers."

"Thanks," I mutter, pushing my way past Taking Back Sunday.

"And Shannon?"

"What?" I say, looking into Sunday's dark eyes as he stares back.

"Happy birthday. Welcome to eighteen."

After going into the bathroom to smoke and calm down during the class break, I make my way over to the gym. There's a bazillion other students waiting to get into the field and people are touching and jostling me as we wait. "What the fuck is going on?" I mutter to myself.

A short girl, who I recognize from the arcade across the street from the high school, smiles at me and starts talking in Spanish.

I scowl at her. "I'm not fucking Mexican."

"Oh," she says. "Sorry." And then she realizes she should be offended by my tone, if not my words, and mutters something else in Spanish which I can only conclude is, *Bitch.*

Well, they've got me pegged. First day of the new semester and I've thrown a fit in the counseling office and insulted someone's culture. I'm going to hell for that last one.

Someone finally unlocks the gate that leads to the athletics field and people start moving forward. The offended girl pushes past me and disappears.

Good going, Shannon. I didn't mean it to come out so rude, but I'm still upset about my counseling session. So yeah, it was rude. But I'm not used to people speaking another language. I'm from Ohio. No one spoke Spanish in my high school there. We had three nationalities—German,

Polish, and Italian. And no one spoke any of those languages either. California has been one long string of culture shocks.

Here at Anaheim they have two major ethnic groups—Filipino and Hispanic. White people are few and far between. On my first day of school last month they had announcements in Tagalog and I seriously thought I was still high from the night before, that's how dumbfounded I was.

I've gotten used to it though. Plus, it helps keep me on the outside and I like being on the outside. There are gangs here like crazy, and girls regularly beat the shit out of each other in the bathrooms.

No one even looks twice at me. Not one of them has ever come up and started shit. Which is more than I can say for my experience in San Diego. Those girls were intense. And that was a rich snobby school. Jill, my sister, was dating a Navy guy at the time and we were living in military housing attached to a wealthy neighborhood. So we had all kinds there. I had to use my tough card more than once.

But here, I'm ignored. Completely, one hundred percent ignored.

I scan the field for the picnic tables, find them, and wander over. "Hey," I say to the two girls sitting on the bench. The Hispanic one has those crutches that attach to the arms. Her legs are bent in a weird way. The African-American one is wearing the thickest coke-bottle glasses I've ever seen and she's holding a white cane between her legs, so I can only conclude she's legally blind. "I'm Shannon. Is this the modified class?"

They both smile at me, the blind girl squinting. "Yeah," the one with the arm crutches says. "I'm Mary and this is Josie. Those guys over there are Lewis and Albert."

Lewis and Albert don't have recognizable disabilities, and they don't even acknowledge me, so I ignore them back. "Is this it?" I ask, looking around.

"This is it," Josie says. "Why are you in here? We haven't had a new student in... what?"

"Two years," Mary says.

"Oh," I say, pointing to my leg. "Bad knee. I faked the excuse, actually. I just don't want to sweat during school, if you know what I mean."

They both laugh and I take a seat next to Mary. "So what do we do? Do we have a teacher?"

"Oh, Mr. Fowler is always late. Sometimes he never even shows up."

"Really?" I get a little excited as I wonder how much that happens. I could skip and go hang out at the arcade.

"We just throw darts or do lawn bowling," Josie says.

I'd laugh, but I don't think she's joking.

"Drake!" a blond guy wearing cargo shorts with a preppy polo shirt yells as he walks up to us. "You Drake?"

"The one and only," I say back.

"OK." He looks over at my new friends. "Hey, girls. Looking good this semester. You know what to do, so choose your weapon." He nods to a box of lawn bowling equipment. "Drake, run three laps around the track."

"I'm not running laps. I've got a bad knee."

Fowler looks up from his roster and scratches his head with a pen. "You're lying. We all know you're lying, we just don't feel like fighting about it. So you're here.

Congratulations on making it into modified PE. Now you're going around that track three times at the start of every class or you're gonna fail. Got it?"

Jesus Christ. I cannot cut a break.

"Josie and I will walk with you," Mary says.

I look at her legs dubiously.

"I can't go fast though," she says, noticing my gaze.

"OK," I say. I'm up for company. I need friends and at least these girls are nice. So the three of us set off to walk laps. They talk incessantly and I half-heartedly listen to them as everyone stares at us. It takes the whole period to walk those three laps, but I can think of millions of worse ways to spend a morning. So I don't complain.

Fowler disappears after attendance. Good to know. I will be cutting this class regularly.

After that my day is economics, then lunch, then English, science, and driver's ed rounds out the day.

Everyone takes driver's ed in tenth grade here, and I'm a senior, so that teacher makes me his assistant. I like driver's ed. I can feel this guy's very low expectations of us the minute he opens his mouth. Plus, the person in the seat next to me is interesting as fuck. She's a tiny Filipino girl named Quinn who is married at fifteen. Last month, that might've shocked me. This month, no way. I'm so out of my league, I just accept it and move on.

Quinn looks like she's in training to be a CEO with her skirt suit and black pumps and she spends the entire class complaining to me about her in-laws as we pretend to watch a movie.

When the final bell rings I make my way to the farthest building on campus where my locker is located. Usually the seniors get lockers in the main building where the offices are. But I'm new, and it was December when I got here, so I'm in no-man's-land.

After that I walk all the way across campus to the front and start heading across the street to the arcade. I have a few acquaintances there from school and I'm just starting to wonder if any of them might have a joint to share when a horn honks and scares me half to death.

Mr. Bowman smiles as he eases his car alongside of me. "Going over to Gilbert, Miss Drake?"

"Shit," I say.

"You forgot?"

"I did. Mr. Bowman, I don't have a ride and I don't even have bus fare—"

"Get in."

"What?" I say, looking around.

"I'll take you. But I can't take you every day, Shannon. You'll have to figure this out."

I rub my head because it's beginning to ache, but if he's offering me an easy way to get there, I might as well take it. So I walk around and get in the passenger side.

"How's your birthday going?" he asks, pulling onto Lincoln Avenue.

"Shitty. I might as well be invisible, that's how much people give a fuck about my birthday."

He laughs and I look over at him. I'd say he's late forties, with blond hair that is just about to go gray, and he's lean and athletic. Not a bad-looking guy for a guidance counselor. And he's tolerant with my fucks. I sorta like that about him.

"It doesn't get any easier, you know."

"I figured as much."

"But I've been in this school for ten years and I rarely see kids with so much potential come through needing help. So I'm taking a personal interest in you."

"Great," I mumble.

"I'm sorry about your sister."

I swallow hard and look straight ahead as we ride down Lincoln.

"It's got to be hard to be uprooted in the middle of your junior year, moved out to California, and then have to switch schools three times in nine months."

"Well," I say, rummaging through my backpack for a cigarette, "it wasn't a picnic, if that's what you're getting at."

"So your brother-in-law?"

"What about him?" I ask, lighting up and blowing my smoke out the window.

"He's…" I look over at Bowman. "Good to you?"

"We tolerate each other."

"And the baby?"

I nod and take another drag. "She's sweet. I love her."

"He's doing OK with her?"

"Why do you want to know?" I ask, getting pissed. "I'm not a chatty girl, Bowman. And I'm private. So if you've got a question, don't beat around the bush. Just ask, and if I want to answer, I will."

"Is he taking care of her, Shannon? We had a meeting about you when you first registered. So everyone knows your situation. And I was asked today to find things out. I'm pretty sure you're a girl who can take care of herself. But a three-month-old baby is something else entirely. If you need help in that area, I want you to come to me. Understand?"

I take another drag of my cigarette and blow rings. "He's doing as well as any guy would if their wife OD'd and left them with an infant. She's in daycare and he works his ass off to pay for it, so that's why he can't take off work to cart my ass around. And besides," I say, suddenly feeling very tired, "as you pointed out this morning, I'm eighteen now. So I'm just lucky he lets me stay at the apartment."

We pull into a parking lot and Bowman stops the car. "OK, just checking. I'll wait and drive you home if you want."

I grab my pack and open the door. "No, thanks. I can hitchhike." And then I slam the door and walk off.

Nosy-ass bastard.

Please, God, I say, feeling my Catholic upbringing coming out. *Just give me a break in here. It's my birthday. I deserve at least one break.*

3

"Mr. Bowman called about you."

"I bet he did," I say dryly.

"We weren't going to have any trig classes this semester, but he put in for a special request for you before Christmas."

"He did?" Jesus Christ. The fucker's been looking out for me.

"Yes," the older woman says from across the counter. "Now here's your official schedule." She holds it out, pointing. "You owe three hundred and fifty dollars."

"What?"

"Sorry, let me explain. Normally you *would* owe three hundred and fifty dollars, but Mr. Bowman got your fee waived this afternoon. It takes a few weeks for that to come in. So if you get a bill in the mail, just ignore it." She smiles at me.

"OK, thank you," I say, taking my schedule and exhaling a long breath. I guess if Bowman has anything to say about it, I'll get that diploma after all. "I'll be back—"

"Wait, wait, wait," the secretary says, just as I'm about to make my big break. "Since the trig class is by special arrangement, you have to set up your schedule with Mr. Alesci. He's down the hallway in room twenty-one. So go do that and then you're free."

She gives me this motherly smile and I wonder how much Bowman told her about me. It's not like I give a shit if people know my sister was a loser who OD'd. I just hate the idea that people are discussing me. It feels like an invasion of privacy.

A crack of thunder scares the both of us and we jump, looking at each other with wide eyes.

"Rainy season," she says.

"Great." I get to look forward to waiting for the bus in the rain. "Which way is twenty-one?"

"Right down there, sweetheart." She points to a grungy hallway off to the left.

"Thanks." I hike my backpack over my shoulder and walk off.

Twenty-one is the last classroom on the left and the door is closed. There's a small window, but all I see are empty desks.

I open the door and walk in to find a man in a suit looking down at some papers on the desk in the front of the room.

"Hey, I'm Shannon Drake. I'm here to set up a time for trig class."

He looks up and all I see are those green eyes from the counseling office this morning. It takes my breath away for a moment. I'm shocked.

"I thought you were gonna ditch me, Shannon."

Just hearing this gorgeous man say my name sends a tingle through my body. "Um..."

"We've met, remember? The counseling office this morning."

"But you weren't..."

"Looking very professional this morning. I know. Sorry. I didn't expect to see my only student." He gives me a small smile and then leans back in his chair, folding his hands behind his neck like he hasn't a care in the world.

His white dress shirt stretches across his muscled chest. And yes, it's muscled because I can see the outline of his pecs through the fabric. He looks almost as delicious dressed up as a teacher as he did as a biker.

"So," he says, releasing his relaxed pose and grabbing a pen from the desk. "Have a seat and let's see how much work we have to do."

I let out a long breath and he averts his eyes and pretends not to notice that I'm nervous and flustered.

I walk forward to the one chair pulled up to the opposite side of the table that acts as a desk. I set my backpack down and pull the chair out, taking a seat. But the table is not that wide and my foot bumps against his when I settle.

I quickly move my feet back and look down so he can't see my blush. *Jesus. Get a hold of yourself, Shannon.*

"So how much do you remember?"

"What?"

"Geometry? I heard you this morning saying it's not your thing. So how much of it *was* your thing?"

I swallow. "Um…"

"That much?"

I shake my head to clear my mind and blurt. "None of it. I cheated."

He bursts out laughing.

"I mean, I didn't cheat for real. But I cheated because I didn't learn a thing. I only memorized things for the tests, and then I went out and partied that night, and then the shit flew right out of my brain with the pot smoke."

Oh. My. God. What the hell did I just say? *Filter, Shannon. Filter.*

His smile grows. "Well, we have our work cut out for us."

"Look, I really don't belong in this class, OK? I'm terrible at math. I don't understand why I can't just take some stupid lower math to get that credit."

He looks down at his paperwork, which to my horror I realize is my file. My fucking file. This hot motherfucker who dresses like a biker and a teacher in the same day has been reading about me.

"Well, you took all AP classes in ninth and tenth grade. Why would we assume you're not smart enough to move forward?"

"Right, but that was two years ago. This is twelfth grade."

He leans back in his chair again, like I'm about to tell him a story and he's interested.

"I don't know why I was put in those AP classes, OK? I'm really not that smart, but most importantly, I'm really not that motivated."

He looks down at my file again and taps it. "Then how did you get an A in AP Biology?" When he looks up, I can tell his mood is changing. He's going from biker who thinks I'm funny to teacher who thinks I'm lying.

"Biology was different."

"How so?"

"Um…" Holy fuck. *Why? Why me, God? It's my birthday and you can't cut me one fucking break?*

"I mean," he continues, "it's not easy. So how was it different?"

"I liked it, I guess. And biology made sense. Math does not make sense."

"Well, that's why you're here with me, Shannon." He doesn't say my name. He growls it. "So maybe you just never had the right teacher."

And then his legs stretch out under the table and rub up against mine.

I have my feet pulled all the way under my chair, so even if I wanted to escape his touch, I can't. So I just sit there, imagining his biker boots as they press up against my Chucks, and pretend it's not happening.

I take a deep breath and exhale. He either takes the hint that I'm overwhelmed, or he didn't even notice in the first place. But either way, he pulls his legs back and the excitement I felt recedes.

"OK, well, you're stuck here. Bowman made it very clear that you need this class to graduate and we've got a lot to cover in one semester. In fact, you should not expect to graduate in the spring. You'll probably get your diploma at the end of the summer."

"What?" Oh, my God. For real, I'm gonna cry now.

"Well," he says, leaning back and placing his hands behind his neck again, "you said you're not motivated so I'm going to assume you're not lying about that. You'll be super lazy and you won't do the work."

I look down and wring my hands in my lap. I wish I could go back one year and decide never to go to California with Jill. I should've just stayed where I was. Maybe asked one of my friends if their parents would let me hang out for a year and a half until graduation. I could've worked at Jackie's dad's Harley shop. Or done secretary work for Ronnie's boss at the welding shop. Jesus, in what world is fuck-up Ronnie my saving grace?

This one, Shannon. It's funny how people you thought were total losers turn out to be stable and good when you see the real world through the eyes of a castaway teenager for nine months.

"Are you going to do the work, Shannon?"

I can't even meet his gaze. I just stare at my wringing hands. "I don't have a choice, do I?"

"You always have a choice. You can choose to be anything you want. Lazy is easy. Skate, you said this morning. You've been skating through life for a while now, haven't you? You're so smart you don't have to study unless you want to. You can get an A on the final and pass the class, so why apply yourself?"

"You have no idea what you're talking about." But I can feel the sting of tears in my eyes and the lump in my throat. I'm really going to cry.

His legs stretch out again, and that feeling from his touch is back. "I know exactly what I'm talking about. I've been you, Shannon."

I look up just as the tears stream down my face. "No one has been me, Mr. Alesci." I growl his name the same way he did mine and it makes him smile. That just pisses me off more. "You have no idea who I am and what I've been through."

"You don't know me either."

"Well, I know who you're not. You're not Shannon Drake. And I don't give a flying fuck what that file says. That file isn't Shannon Drake either."

"Noted," he says, ignoring my tears. "If you want to do the work and graduate on time, we meet every day for the rest of the semester."

"I can't," I say, and then I really do start crying. I'm talking sobs. Everything that's happened to me today—hell, the past nine months—comes pouring out in front of this man who has no right to be asking me these things.

"Why can't you?" he asks, his voice gentler. Softer. "You're smart. I can tell." He reaches for a handkerchief in his suit coat pocket and hands it to me.

I take it and start wiping my face.

"Why can't you, Shannon?"

I suddenly want to tell him everything. All the bullshit that's happened to me. But once I let it out, it will never go back in. And I'm not ready for that. I'll die if that happens.

"Bowman mentioned something about not having a ride. Do you need a ride?"

I picture Bowman driving me to Gilbert every day. All the pressing questions, all the explanations he'll be probing me for. All the privacy he'll be invading. "No, that's not it. I have a ride."

"Then what?" Alesci asks.

I sniff and get myself together. "Never mind," I say, standing up and grabbing my backpack. "I'll be here every day."

I walk out. No, really, I run out. I run right past the front desk and burst through the doors like something is chasing me and if I stop, I will die.

It's raining pretty good when I get outside and I'm grateful for it. No one can see my tears as I walk across the parking lot and head down the street towards Lincoln. There's a bus stop there at the corner. And even though I lied to Bowman this morning about not having money, I have two dollars.

Jason, my brother-in-law, leaves me five dollars a day to eat and I still have two left over from lunch. He never buys groceries, just formula for little Olivia. She's a good baby, I think. I don't have any experience with babies, but she sleeps a lot. Any time someone asks about her, that's the one thing Jason says. *She's a good sleeper.*

Those are magic words in the baby world, I guess. New parents are supposed to long for sleep.

When Jill got pregnant we were living with Michael in Navy housing down in San Diego. She never married him, thank God, because it wasn't his baby. It was Jason's. Jason came over one night and they had this huge fight in front of the whole neighborhood. And if you've never seen Navy housing, it's packed with families. Just people everywhere. Kids playing, soldiers hanging out in driveways, wives gossiping like crazy.

And let me tell you, the night Jason showed up at Michael's house was one for the books. I bet that neighborhood is still talking about it.

Jill, to put it lightly, was drama. Nothing but drama. I'm so sick of drama, but that's my life too. I can't seem to escape it. And today is proof. I just bawled in front of a complete stranger over math.

But I was a quiet kind of drama. People knew I was heading in the wrong direction, but it wasn't so obvious. Jill was obvious. So when our mom, who had us really close together and really late in life, died, it was Jill, at the tender age of eighteen, who took over.

I guess the social workers figured I was seventeen, so not worth their time. And Jill jumped through hoops to keep me at home. Our house and car were paid off, so we could get by with her job as a checker at the grocery store down the street.

But no one predicted that she'd sell the house, pack us up in the five-year-old family sedan, and take off for California. It was an adventure, she said. And even though I wanted to stay so bad, how could I? She sold our house. I didn't have anywhere to go except with her.

Biggest mistake of my life, I realize now. Because she's dead from drugs, I'm stuck living with her husband, and her baby will grow up with no mother.

I get to the bus stop and of course, it's not the kind with a shelter over it. This is sunny California. Who needs protection from the rain here?

I'm soaked, anyway. Who cares?

So I just stand there, looking down Lincoln and praying for a bus.

A motorcycle roars up and stops right in front of me. I squint my eyes and then the rider flips the tinted visor up on his black helmet and Jesus Christ. It's Alesci.

"Get on," he says.

"What?" I look around, bewildered.

"Get on the bike, Shannon."

He scoots forward and I have a moment where I think I might tell him where to shove his bike. But... I can be home taking a warm shower in five minutes if I do get on.

My leg swings over, and then he takes his helmet off, reaches around, and pushes it down on my head. The world dulls as the padding inside the helmet squishes against my hair, and I let out a long breath when he gives it some throttle and we take off, the wind whipping against my wet clothes and the rain stinging my bare arms like little bullets.

He slows when we get about half a mile down the road and then turns into a bank that looks like it closed down a decade ago. We come to a stop under the shelter they have over the drive-through, and then he cuts the engine and gets off the bike.

"What the fuck are we doing?" But I realize I'm talking to the visor of the helmet, and lift it off my head. "What are you doing?" I ask again.

"It's not safe to ride in the rain, Shannon." He says this like I'm a child and all the things need explaining. "Besides, I only have one helmet."

"Oh," I say, looking at the helmet in my hands. I thrust it towards him. "Thanks. I can wait it out here."

He takes the helmet, but instead of putting it on and riding away, he sets it down on his seat and walks over to the little curb up against the bank building. He slides down the wall, stretching his legs out in front of him like he did under the table at school. That excited feeling he gave me comes back.

"What are you doing?" I ask, hugging my arms to my chest. I'm soaking wet and my shirt is white and plastered up against my skin. I'm one hundred percent certain my bra is showing through the fabric.

"Waiting with you. I'm not leaving you here alone."

"Why not? I'm not helpless."

But he ignores me and tabs something on his phone. He sets his phone down on the concrete and takes off his leather jacket. It's black, and old-looking, like he's been wearing it his whole life. He holds it out to me and asks, "You cold?"

I'm freezing. I'm so cold my teeth might start chattering. And besides, I don't want him to be looking at my bra through my shirt. So I reach out and take the jacket and slip my arms inside.

It's warm. And heavy.

It makes me sigh and I wander across the small distance that separates us and take a seat next to him. Not too close. He makes me nervous. That's a new feeling for me. Usually I'm the one making guys nervous.

I rummage around in my backpack and pull out a cigarette, offering Alesci one. He shakes his head and leans back against the brick wall. I light up my cigarette and blow out a puff of smoke into the cold air.

The silence hangs there between us and I start shuffling my feet, unable to figure out what's going on. Should he be offering me rides? Should I be accepting them? Should he be allowed to be so hot and my teacher at the same time? Does he always wear a suit under his leather jacket?

"I've known Bowman for a long time," he says.

"That right? Did he ask you to be my teacher?"

"Called me up last month and said he had a job for me. I'm between jobs right now. Well…" He laughs. "Technically I'm supposed to be writing my dissertation for my PhD. I go to UCLA and after ten years of work, the shit is about to pay off. All I gotta do is write up my contribution to science and I'm on my way. But I figure you're a good excuse to procrastinate, because while math might be my thing, writing is not."

"UCLA, huh?" I say. Last semester I worked in the office at Anaheim because my school in San Diego said I had a ton of credits and only had to go to school half a day. So at Anaheim I worked in the library first period shelving books and the office second period sorting mail into little cubbies. One day a catalog came for the art school at UCLA and I put it in my backpack and took it home.

I've never thought about college. No one has ever talked to me about college. Not even my guidance counselors back home.

But that catalog was so pretty I had to have it. So I stole it. And I read it cover to cover that same night. I've always wanted to be an artist. That's why I was in that alternative school back in Ohio. I was taking graphic design and learning Photoshop, and that's the closest I've came so far.

But UCLA art school. God.

"What are you taking at UCLA?" I ask, genuinely interested.

He laughs. And it's such a warm, hearty laugh, I want to bottle it up and keep it with me for all the days ahead that I will be sad. "Computer engineering with a concentration in physics," he says.

"Jesus," I say. "If they make me take physics, I'm quitting."

He laughs again and this time I catch a little gleam in his green eyes. "It's not really my thing, either. My thing is astronomy. But I have a plan that ties it all together. Now I just need to sell people on it."

Astronomy. That is so cool. "Do you think you will?" I turn my body to face him and wait for his answer. "Sell people on your plan?"

But he just shrugs. "Dunno. I did my best, so whatever."

"How do you know Bowman?"

"I was his first student when he came to Anaheim ten years ago."

"You're twenty…?"

"Eight," he says, smiling at me like he's hungry.

Jeeeesus. Why does my teacher have to be so hot? Ten years older than me. I almost can't stop staring. I have to force myself to look away and take a drag off my cigarette.

"He helped me get into CU right after high school. I was sorta like you. Smart, but unmotivated. He motivated me."

"CU?"

"University of California."

"Oh. I'm not up on all that college stuff."

"You should be."

"Why? It's not like I'm ever going."

"Why not?"

"Um." I laugh. "I'm broke, number one."

"They have scholarships. But you have to apply."

"My grades are terrible. And the occasional A in biology won't cover that fact up."

"There's lots of ways to go to college, Shannon."

"Maybe it's just not for me," I say, irritated.

"Maybe you have no idea what's good for you."

"And you do?"

He shrugs again. "I know you can do trig."

"Like hell. I'm not sure why everyone thinks I'm so smart here, but back in Ohio I was nothing but average. So you people either have very low standards or you have no idea what mediocrity looks like."

He laughs. "Mediocre people don't use the word 'mediocrity,' Shannon."

I sigh and take another drag. "I'm tired of talking about this. I'd rather just be invisible, thanks. Bowman should mind his own business and ignore me like everyone else."

"Who's ignoring you?" He chuckles. "I can't imagine you get ignored much. You're like a little explosion in a bottle."

"You'd be wrong. Everyone ignores me at this school. Some girl started talking Spanish to me this morning. She just assumed I was Hispanic because I have brown hair. And I've seen and even talked to her at least half a dozen times, yet she never saw me." I take a drag. "It pissed me off too. Invisible, that's what I am. I guess I should get used to it."

"Your call," he says, standing. Just then a yellow cab pulls under the shelter and comes to a stop next to his bike. "Your ride's here anyway."

I get up and wipe the stones off my ass, but it's no use. I'm still soaked. Alesci walks over to the cab and talks to the driver through the window. He turns to me, opens the back door of the cab, and waves me in.

"This is me?" I ask, dumbfounded. "I don't have enough to pay for a cab."

"I paid with a credit card online."

"Oh." He planned this pretty thoroughly. I start to slip the jacket off and give it back, but he stops me with a warm hand on my shoulder.

"Keep it on, Shannon. I can see your tits through that bra. And next time you wear a white shirt, check to see if it's gonna rain before you leave the house without a jacket."

My whole face heats up and I'm quite positive it's bright red.

"You're good for the jacket, right?"

I nod and swallow hard.

"I'm gonna be seeing a lot of you, Shannon Drake. There's no way in hell you'll be invisible to me."

I don't even know what to say. So I just slip into the cab and lean back against the seat and wonder why my heart is beating so fast.

"Mateo," he says, leaning down into the cab, his face so close to mine I can feel the heat of his breath.

"What?" I whisper.

"My name," he says. "Mateo Alesci. Happy birthday, Shannon. See you tomorrow." And then he closes the door and pounds twice on the roof to signal the cabbie to leave.

I'm still repeating his name in my head fourteen blocks later when the cab pulls up in front of my apartment.

And then it hits me. He knows where I live. He knows everything about me because he has my file.

Our building is a collection of one-story apartments in a u-shape, centered on a grassy quad. There are only about fifteen of them. There's an alley on the other side of the laundry room building where people have small garages. The 5 freeway is less than fifty yards from where I stand on the curb, and less than twenty feet from my bedroom window.

It is a constant source of white noise that I have gotten used to. It's a comforting hum in a life that should be empty silence.

I am not even halfway across the grass, heading towards our corner apartment, and I can hear the baby. The windows are open and she is loud. I know I should go inside and help Jason, but I haven't eaten since lunch and I still have two dollars in my pocket. So I keep walking past our front window, thankful that the curtains are drawn, and slip into the alley. Bill's Burgers is just on the other side of the freeway and they have ninety-nine cent sliders for happy hour. I have about fifteen minutes to make the deadline, so I jog, my backpack slapping with the rhythm of my feet.

I'm still wet, but the heat is on and it rushes past my face when I enter the restaurant.

"Hey, Shan," Jose, the owner, says from behind the kitchen counter. He says this even though there are about a dozen people milling around and waiting for service or take-out.

Every head swings to look at me and I can't look down at my feet fast enough.

"The usual?" he asks.

I nod and slip to the back where I sit at a two-seater table that no one ever wants because it's right next to the bathroom. But I like it. I like everything that is less desirable. I like to be where other people aren't.

I run the day through my head. The meeting this morning feels so far away. But one thing that still feels very close is the heat of Mateo's breath when he whispered his name in my ear.

And he was looking at my tits.

It's so inappropriate.

A few minutes later Jose comes with my sliders and sets the red plastic basket down, along with a Diet Pepsi, which I can't afford. "Thanks," I say, hunching down into myself. I set my two dollars on the table and he pushes it back towards me.

"You keep it. I made this for some lady who got an emergency and walked out before picking them up."

"Liar," I say. But I smile.

"How is that no-good bastard?"

He's talking about Jason. They grew up together. In fact, Jason has a lot of childhood friends in this area of Anaheim. This is where he grew up. He even went to Anaheim High too.

I envy people who have a whole community of history surrounding them. I wish every day that I was still at home in my familiar neighborhood.

"He's OK." I force a smile and look up as I take a bite and talk with my mouth full. "Mmmm. You have the best greasy burgers in town, Jose."

He shoots me with his finger. "Tell everyone you know." He walks off when his wife, Maria, starts yelling for him to get back in the kitchen.

My mind wanders back to Mateo. I will have to see him every day if I go back.

Should I go back? Is a stupid piece of paper worth all this trouble?

I'm not sure yet. So I just chew my food and drink my DP, and pretty soon, I'm out of reasons why I should stay here.

The rain has stopped when I walk back home. And the baby is silent when I grab the door handle and give it a turn.

Jason is sitting on the couch watching TV, his feet kicked up on a bright blue trunk that acts as a coffee table. "Where the fuck have you been?"

He's angry, and drunk. Well, maybe not drunk. But he's definitely drinking because there's two bottles of Corona on the side table next to the remote. They're both empty.

I sit on a chair across from the couch. "So it turns out..." But then the words get stuck in my throat. It's so complicated, way too complicated to answer in a few sentences, so I just give up. "I was getting high with Phil." It's so much easier to lie.

"Hmmm," Jason says. "Must be nice to fuck off all day and have no responsibilities. Whose coat is that? You have a boyfriend now?"

I don't say anything to that. Phil is another childhood friend who lives all the way down the alley in a little house across West Street. He's a small-time dealer. Pot mostly. And he sells it by the joint, so he's my kind of dealer— affordable. Plus, he likes me and smokes me out whenever I go over there.

"You're gonna need to get a job, Shannon. I can't pay for you anymore."

I nod. "OK. I'll look tomorrow." All I want is to go to my room and collapse on my hard futon. It feels like sleeping on concrete, but things could be worse. I could be sleeping on the disgusting twenty-year-old carpet instead.

"So where were you really? Because I called down to Phil's and you weren't there."

"I don't want to talk about it."

"Poor baby," he says, his words rumbling out of his chest. "You're eighteen now," he continues, looking me up and down in a way that makes me uncomfortable. He makes me uncomfortable a lot. He came on to me once back in San Diego, but he was very drunk and the next day he pretended it never happened. "Legal."

"What's that mean?" I don't look like Jill at all. She had blonde hair and blue eyes and I have brown hair and brown eyes, so if he thinks I'm her replacement, he's wrong in every way I can think of.

Jason gets up from the couch and walks towards the small kitchen in the front of the apartment, his fingertips dragging along my knee as he passes. I hiss in a breath but he pretends not to notice. My eyes track him as he grabs another bottle of beer from the fridge, then pops the top off and throws it into the sink. That's when I notice several more empty bottles on the counter.

He takes a long drag on his beer and then walks back over to me, stopping right in front of my chair. He places both hands on the arms and leans down. "You're prettier than her, you know that."

"Well, she's dead," I say back. Emotionless. "So it's not that hard."

He reaches out and the back of his knuckles sweep down my cheek. My foot comes up automatically and I kick him hard in the chest, sending him reeling backwards. He must be drunker than I figured, because he crashes against the trunk, spilling over a vase with dead flowers left over from Jill's funeral last month.

The baby starts screaming in the other room and I see the rage in Jason's eyes. "You fucking bitch!" he snarls, trying to get up.

But I'm out of there. I bolt for the door and pull it open, but he's behind me, slamming it shut again. His drunken slowness has no dampening effect on his rage. He spins me around and punches me in the cheek, good enough to see stars.

My rage is out of control. "I hit back, motherfucker." I grab his shoulders and bring my knee right into his balls.

He steps back just enough to let me turn and open the door again. I push on the screen and step outside, thankful that I had the good sense to never take my backpack off.

There's a woman across the grassy area shoving a key into her door. She turns and I close my eyes and grit my teeth.

Jason appears behind me, but he must see the same thing I do, because he says nothing, just slams the door closed behind me.

"Shannon?"

How is it that I've lived here for one month and everybody seems to know my name?

I ignore her. She's a cop who just moved in two weeks ago. But she parks her squad car on the street, not back in the alley. So I see her getting in and out of it all the time when she comes home during a shift.

"Shannon?" she repeats.

I make for the little path that leads to the alley next to the laundry room, but she catches me by the leather jacket and I spin around and shrug her off. "Don't touch me." I growl it.

She lets go. "Is everything OK?"

"Does everything fucking look OK?" I snarl it this time. But I don't wait for an answer because my face is stinging from the hit I took and I'm pretty sure it's red and getting ready to bruise. I take off down the alley, walking as fast as I can without running.

Eighteen had better improve fast. Because if this is what it's gonna be like for the rest of my life, then what is the point?

I don't have many options. I could go to the arcade across the street from the high school. That's only two blocks away and the guy who runs it, Mark, another friend of Jason's, is cool. He always gets me high when I go there and it's slow.

Why are all Jason's friends so nice and he's such a raging asshole?

But all the kids from school hang out at the arcade in the evenings and I don't want to see anyone right now. So I go to Phil's. It's a dumb move because if Jason wants to go looking for me that will be the first stop.

But again, limited options.

So I trudge up the alley, my Chucks soaking wet as I splash through the leftover puddles, and cross West Street. Phil's car isn't in the driveway, so I know he's not home. But I knock on the door anyway. Desperate times and all.

The locks disengage and I have half a second of excitement about being wrong, but then I look up into the face of Taking Back Sunday.

Jesus Christ. No breaks, huh?

"Hey," he says. "Cage the Elephant. Nice jacket. Didn't have that on this morning." I hear lots of rowdy voices inside as I wonder if he saw who *was* wearing this jacket this morning.

"Is Phil here?"

Sunday shakes his head. "Mexico for a few days. I'm watching the dog."

"Oh," I say, surprised. "I've never seen you here before."

"Ditto. He's my cousin. Want to come in? We're passing a joint."

I sigh, look over my shoulder at the street, and then shrug. He moves aside and opens the door, and I slip past him, my jacket brushing against his arm.

Everyone stops talking for a moment as I log their faces. I recognize most of them. A group of kids from school who also hang out at the arcade. I realize now that I've seen Sunday before. But these are not my people, not that I even have people here, and I've never really talked to them.

"Shannon," a tall girl standing in the kitchen says. She's got short jet-black hair and her eyes are thick with black eyeliner. "Miss Bad Day, huh?"

I squint my eyes at her. "What?"

"Danny," she says, nodding to Sunday, who is now standing next to me. "He told us about your epic tantrum in the office this morning. Way to go, bitch. I hear the fucks were flying and everyone was too afraid to stop you."

"Who—"

"That's Rocky," Sunday says. "And that's Greg, and Tim, and Matt." Sunday points to the three guys passing the joint in the small living room.

"Wanna hit?" Greg asks. He's got light, curly brown hair that ends at the top of his shoulders and a kind face.

I shake my head and look around, feeling more helpless than I have in a very long time. "Can I use your bathroom?" I ask Sunday.

"You know where—"

I do. So I just walk off and make my way down the hallway, taking a left at the end and slipping inside, locking the door behind me.

I can hear them whisper so I turn on the faucet to drown out the hum of gossip and splash water on my face. When I look in the mirror there sure as shit is a red mark on my cheek. I touch it with my fingertips and will it to go away, but it doesn't. It practically darkens as I watch, my hands propping me up on each side of the small, white, pedestal sink.

"Shannon?" Sunday's soft voice is accompanied by a knock. "You OK?"

Silence from me. I feel a little paralyzed. I'm so not OK. "Yeah," I say, clearing my throat. "Be right out."

"You want a dry t-shirt? I have a clean one if you want it."

"Um."

"It's outside the door."

I turn the faucet off and listen to his retreating footsteps, and then open the door as quietly as I can and grab the shirt. It's another black concert shirt, but this one says *My Chemical Romance*.

I take my shirt off and drape it over the towel rack to dry, and then slip the new one on. It's way too big, but it feels nice. I stare at myself for another few minutes, desperate to find a way out of this day. But I'm not a coward and I'm done hiding in here, so I gather myself and walk back out to the living room.

It's empty.

Except Sunday.

"Where'd everyone go?"

He smiles at me. "You look like…"

"Hell?"

That gets a small laugh out of him. But he shakes his head. "Nah, just tired. And like you're not in the mood for company."

"Yeah, I should go."

"You don't have to," he says, pointing to the TV. "You can stay and watch a movie if you want."

And because he seems nice and I have nowhere to go but home, I plop down on the couch and stare at the screen.

He doesn't say another word. Not one question, not one comment, not one attempt at conversation.

And I am so fucking grateful for my invisibility, I fall asleep on the couch exhausted at the end of a very bad day that I will never be able to forget.

Because it's a milestone.

The first day of my adult life was filled with disappointments, admonishments, and a hit to the face.

But also an opportunity and this guy, Sunday, who does not even know me, but who knew just what to do to make it better.

Just call me an optimist. Always looking for that silver lining.

The next morning I'm so disoriented, it takes me whole minutes to come to terms with the realization that I'm not in my own bed, that Rocky girl is talking to me, and Sunday is cooking something that smells delicious.

"What?" I say, looking up at Rocky.

"Your bruise," she says, pointing to my face.

I touch it and wince. "What about it?"

"Do you want me to cover it?" She holds up a clear bag of makeup. "It's not too bad."

"Done this before, huh?"

She smiles with a shrug.

"Sure."

I use the bathroom, smile back at Sunday when he smiles at me, and then plop down at the small kitchen table and look longingly at the food in front of me as Rocky makes me pretty.

Sunday watches. I can't figure out if I like that he's watching or if I don't.

"Are you going to school today?" he asks.

I check my face with a compact mirror and then hand it back to Rocky with a thank you. "I think I have to."

"Graduation and shit, right?" He has a great smile, I realize. Friendly. His hair is very dark, but he's not Hispanic. Ditto for Rocky. They both have very dark eyes and when I look directly into Sunday's, he's staring at me.

45

"Hey, are you two related?"

"Twins," they say together.

"Obviously not identical," Sunday says. "I'm so much better-looking."

Rocky halfheartedly punches him and then gets up to grab some more bacon from the counter before snatching her backpack from the coffee table and walking to the door. "I'll see you there, Danny. Gotta meet Tim."

"Yeah, bye," Sunday absently says. His eyes never leave mine. "You need a ride to school then? I live back there," he says, thumbing behind his shoulder to indicate behind us.

"Oh," I say. "I was wondering where you got this shirt from."

"Phil's my cousin," he says. "Rocky and I have lived in the apartment above the garage since last summer when we turned eighteen."

I wince at the word.

He stays silent for a long second. "I get it, you know."

"Get what?" I ask through a mouthful of bacon.

"The bad day."

"Oh, that." I chew and swallow. "Yeah, well, it's behind me now, so bygones and all that good shit."

"You're gonna go far with that attitude, Daydreams."

"Daydreams?" I ask.

"You called me Sunday last night."

"I did not."

"You woke up about three am asking for water. And you said, *Thanks, Sunday.* And I said, *Who the fuck is Sunday?* And you said, *You, dumbass.* And then you grabbed my t-shirt and pulled me down, close to your face, and said—"

"I did not do any of that," I say, laughing.

"Then how do I know you call me Sunday?"

"I don't... know."

He leans across the table, his face getting so close to mine I have a shock of fear that he might try to kiss me. And then he whispers, "Because you said it, Daydreams."

He leans back into his chair again and I just stare straight ahead for a few moments. All I can do is blink silently.

"And I was gonna call you Elephant, but—" He shrugs.

My smile is big. "I like Daydreams better."

"My favorite song by them," he says. "*Cigarette Daydreams.* 'Youuuu were only seventeen. So sweet—with a mean streak.'"

I laugh.

"'Nearly brought me to my knees.'"

"Oh, my God."

He stops singing. "But you're eighteen now. So fuck. I'm a day late, aren't I?"

I take a deep breath and let that little thrill wash over me. That thrill that says you might've just met someone special. "Nah, you're right on time, Sunday."

He stands up and get his keys, then grabs my backpack off the floor. "Ready?"

"Sure," I say, grabbing Alesci's leather jacket—thankful Sunday didn't mention it again— and fall into step with him. We leave by the back door and he backs an older-model Acura out while I wait in the driveway, since the garage is too small to get in the passenger side.

I open the door and slide in next to him. The car is not new, but he takes good care of it and the leather is soft to the touch.

"I'd put some music on," he says, flipping the car around so he can get out of the driveway without backing into the street. "But then you'd have no reason to talk to me."

I shake my head. He's nice. Built like a quarterback, I remind myself. And he has a handsome face. "It's a two-minute ride to school. Not much to say."

"You can start with something like… what happened last night?"

I frown.

"Or not. You'll tell me eventually though."

"How do you know that?" I watch him drive, his eyes straight ahead. He didn't shave this morning, so he's got more stubble than he did yesterday.

"Because you're stuck with me now, Daydreams. I like you."

I laugh and look out the window. "Thanks, by the way."

"What for?" he asks, pulling up to the stop sign at Lincoln Avenue.

"Rescuing me."

"Ha." He laughs. "I don't think you needed a rescue, Shannon." When he says my name my stomach flutters. "You just needed a hand up, that's all."

"Well, thanks for the offer. I don't get many."

"Huh. Could've fooled me. Bowman gave you one yesterday. But maybe it was just crushed between all the kicks in the face, so you missed it?"

He looks over at me and then back to the road. A few seconds later we're pulling into a parking space, tons of kids and cars all around us. We sit there in silence for a few moments, just the ticking of the engine after he turns it off. "I'll take you home, too. And I sit on the wall at lunch." He gets out of the car and I follow. We stare at each other over the hood for a few moments. "Don't ditch me, Daydreams. I like you."

And then he walks off.

"Hey, Sunday?" I call. He turns around, a huge shit-eating grin on his face as he walks backwards. "Did you see these guys in concert?" I ask, pulling on the shoulder of the *My Chemical Romance* t-shirt I'm wearing.

"What? You think I shop at Hot Topic or something? Where else would I get it?" He laughs and turns back around, a few other boys joining him as they walk onto campus.

No. He's not a day late all. He's most definitely right on time.

Day two of second semester goes pretty much like day one, except for the first-period smackdown by Bowman. Fowler doesn't even bother showing for PE, so Mary and Josie and I walk our laps, slow as sloths, until the bell rings. I sit through economics thinking about how Sunday and I can be in the same grade and yet I have no classes with him.

At lunch I'm nervous. I'm not sure why—he told me to find him. Practically ordered me not to ditch him. But still, my stomach flutters like crazy when I approach the wall.

It's not a wall. Well, it sorta is. It's a circle, like some kind of giant brick fire pit, but it's got benches and there's no fire pit in the middle. And it's not all filled with white kids, it just looks that way because everyone is dressed up grunge. Flannels, army jackets, combat boots, Chucks, Docs, ripped jeans, ripped shirts, tattoos, piercings, metal bands, pink hair, blue hair, black hair, black clothes, and lots of chains as jewelry.

We are Hot Topic.

I almost laugh at that.

But we are not all white. Every ethnicity here is represented because people—no matter where they are from, what color their skin, or any of those other bullshit identifiers—people congregate with their tribes.

These are my people. I knew the very first day last month that if I found friends in this school, this is where I'd find them.

Sunday greets me when I approach. Introduces me, includes me. Even puts his arm around me once. Fleetingly. I suspect it was some kind of secret signal to another guy that I'm not available. That even though he and I are not together, he's claimed me.

I'm surprisingly OK with that.

But when the bell rings and he leans down to—I don't know, kiss me?—I put my hand on his chest. "I like you," I say. "But I'm not looking. So…"

"So?" he says.

"So if that's what you're after, I'm gonna disappoint you."

He takes my backpack off my shoulder and says, "I'll walk you to class."

The rest of the day flies by with my head in a fog. What is he doing? Does he want to be friends? He wasn't mad when I stopped his kiss. *If* he was going to kiss me. I think he was.

At the end of the day I grab Alesci's jacket from my locker and head to the front of the school. Sunday is there, waiting right where Bowman picked me up yesterday.

"'Bout time," he says, taking my backpack and giving the jacket a weird look. *Please don't ask me about it. Please, please, please.* "Wanna come over? I got a couple hours before work."

"Oh, I can't," I say. "I have night school down at Gilbert."

"Need a ride?"

I nod, wincing at how dependent I am on people these days. When we get to his car, he opens my door for me. "Thank you," I say.

He just smiles, gets in his side, and holds out his hand. "Give me your phone."

"What?"

"Your phone. So I can call you and give you my number."

I fish around in my backpack for my phone and hand it to him. He doesn't even remark on how old it is, how the screen is cracked, or how all the numbers are practically rubbed off on the outdated keys. He calls himself, then presses end, adds his name to my contacts, and hands it back.

"Call me when you're done there and I'll come get you."

"I thought you had to work?"

He shrugs and starts the car. "My boss is flexible."

As soon as I'm out of Sunday's car my mind immediately goes back to last night with Mateo. It's like a switch flips. But his motorcycle isn't in the parking lot, and I realize I have another class to go to before his.

I sit through science with my leg bouncing the entire time. Science isn't a class. It's a room with about eight kids who have a textbook and do tests. You can do them all open-book and get a C, or do the work and study and go for an A. I opt for open-book and complete four tests in two hours.

The teacher, who never even introduces himself to me, shoots me looks each time I turn one in. "Trying to get them all done in one day, Drake?"

"Yes," I say. "I have very little control over my life at the moment. I take it where I can get it."

He leaves me alone after test three.

When the class is finally dismissed I am consumed with thoughts of Mateo. We didn't even set up a time last night. What if he's not here? Where am I supposed to go? Should I go to the office and ask?

But in the end, he is sitting at that little table desk in room twenty-one. He's not wearing a suit. Jesus fuck. His plain white t-shirt stretches across his chest just like the dress shirt did yesterday. And his bare arms are covered in tattoos. His dark hair is neither long nor short, and he's got a little curl that falls down onto his forehead.

I want very badly to touch that little curl of hair.

"You're late," he says.

"I am?"

He nods up to the clock, which reads five minutes after five.

"Was I supposed to be here at five? Because you never said yesterday."

"Here's your book," he says, leaning around to grab a textbook and dropping it on the table with a loud thump. "And here," he says, repeating the action, "is your workbook. You have homework every night. On Tuesdays and Thursdays we meet at five and stay until seven. Mondays, Wednesdays, and Fridays we'll meet at five and stay until seven. On the weekends—"

"Weekends?"

He looks up at me, those green eyes burning. He's pissed about something, I realize. "We did agree on every day?"

"But you never said anything about the weekends."

"We can meet at my house on the weekends."

"What?"

"My *house*, Shannon. Do you prefer mornings or mornings?"

I don't know what to say. This guy, he's like a bulldozer who runs me over. "I don't think I can do weekends."

"You can," he says, nodding. "Now sit down and tell me what you know about integers." His legs stretch out under the table. They scissor between mine. My eyes dart up to look at him. "Problem?" he asks.

I blink.

"No? Then read the first paragraph on page eight and tell me what you think it means."

I look down at my book.

His legs move against mine. Rubbing back and forth. What the fuck?

"Read it, Shannon."

I swallow and begin. I read for whole minutes about numbers on a number line. Shit any second grader should know, but authors feel compelled to repeat at the beginning of each textbook. I stop at the end of the page and look up.

He smiles. "Keep going."

"This is dumb."

"How so?"

"The other class I'm taking just lets me take tests. Can't I just take tests?"

"The other teacher in that other class doesn't give a shit about you."

"And you do?"

"I'm here, right?"

"He's there, right?"

"He didn't give you a jacket to wear in the rain last night. He didn't pick you up, take you somewhere dry, and buy you a cab ride home."

"No, but that's not how most teachers behave, Mr.—"

"Mateo."

I just stare at him. What the fuck is his game?

"Say it," he says. "Say my name."

I swallow down the confusion. "Mateo?"

He sighs, letting out a long breath of air. And then he leans over the table, grabs my face, and kisses me.

I am so stunned, I don't move. But his mouth demands something. Cooperation, or interaction, or submission, I'm not sure.

But I do kiss him back, I'm very sure of that.

He fists my hair, making me stand up, and then his lips break free as he walks around the table, keeping hold of my hair while he does it.

I look over my shoulder, my heart beating fast and my breathing coming out in small gasps. "The door is open," I whisper, almost in a panic.

He ignores me, just grabs my breast, pulls me towards him, threads his fingers up my scalp so he can fist my hair again, and takes what he wants. My mouth.

I give in. I feel helpless. Weightless. Powerless.

When he breaks the kiss, I feel like I might pass out.

"Where were you last night?"

"What?" I ask, taken by surprise.

"Where were you last night, Shannon? I know you weren't home."

"How do you know that?"

He leans down to kiss me again, but this time his teeth nip the sensitive skin.

I let out a small whimper. "The door," I say, trying to pull away. "Someone will see us!"

"Everyone leaves at five." He kisses me again and then pulls back, staring down at me like I've done something wrong. "Where were you last night?"

"At a friend's house."

He pushes me backwards, trying to make me lie back on the desk. It's slow and not at all harsh. But he makes it clear that I *will* be bending backwards for him. I give in and let my back rest on the table.

He unbuckles his belt.

"What are you doing?" I ask, really in a panic.

"Fucking you," he says. And in my head I imagine that he says it mean, or rude, or condescending. But he doesn't. He says it like it's already happened.

"You can't fuck me."

"I can if you don't stop me." He grabs my hand and places it over the hard bulge under his jeans, rubbing, moving my fingers back and forth along his shaft. His eyes narrow with pleasure and then he lets go, but I continue.

"Yeah," he mumbles, his attention back to the task of setting himself free. And a moment later his cock springs out. Long and thick, the head swollen and the tip ready. He pulls a condom out of his back pocket and rolls it down his shaft.

I gulp air.

"Unbutton your jeans, Shannon."

I do. I unbutton them. I unzip them before he even asks. And then I lift my hips up so he can drag them down my thighs. He leaves them on, bunched up at my knees, and then he lifts my legs up towards my shoulders, dips his head under and licks my pussy.

I almost come immediately.

"Are you a virgin?"

"No," I whisper.

"Good," he whispers back. "Because I don't have the patience for that."

He sucks on me, teasing my clit, swirling it around in little circles. It's so intense my hand flies down to his head, almost ready to push him off me.

But he stops for a moment, and says, "Be still. And don't come yet."

I moan. I don't know if I can control it. I've never had a problem achieving an orgasm, but I swear, I don't ever remember being so turned on before. It's the door, I think. The open door. I imagine myself walking by, getting a glimpse of his muscled body taking me this way on a makeshift desk in the middle of a classroom.

Wetness pools between my legs and he hums, "Mmmmm," as his tongue does that dance.

He swipes over my clit and I grab his hair. Handfuls of it in my fists. I don't know what comes over me except that I'm consumed with need. I push on his head, urging him to go deeper. And then his fingers are there and… and…

I just explode.

I'm not a screamer, I swear, but I scream.

He laughs, pulls back, pumps his dick a few times, and then enters me. And as rough as it was a few seconds ago, that's how soft it is now. Long, slow movements. In and out, the friction of his cock spreading me. I just don't know what to do except lie there and enjoy it.

He leans over the table and I can smell him. He smells like motorcycle oil, and leather, and sweat, and desire. He smells like me too. He smells like a man.

"I'm gonna come on that shirt," he says. "Because it's not yours."

And before I can say no, he does. He pulls out, rips the condom off, and comes all over the t-shirt that isn't even mine.

We look at each other for a few seconds and then he lets out a breath and pulls away.

I swallow down the realization of what we just did as he tucks his dick away and buckles his pants. He combs his hand over his messed-up hair and then looks me in the eye as I lie there on the desk, my legs still spread open before him. "I've been wanting to do that for a month."

It takes several seconds for that sentence to register. "What?"

He takes my hand and pulls me up, then hikes my jeans back up my legs. "OK, now that we got that out of the way, we still gotta work. Go clean up and get your ass back here. You have three minutes."

"What?"

"Now, Shannon."

9

My phone dings in my backpack while I'm in the bathroom.

Sunday: What time?

Jesus Christ. I managed to stay away from boys for a whole month and then in one day, I've got two guys. It's not my fault, and I should not lead Sunday on, but I need to get out of here. No way I'm staying.

Shannon: Now.

Sunday: On my way.

I can't even go back in that classroom. I cannot believe I just let Mateo fuck me like that. Slut.

Two knocks on the door, and then Mateo peeks his head in. "Let's go."

I shake my head at him. "No. My boyfriend is coming to get me."

He stares at me. Expressionless. Several seconds flash by. "You do not have a boyfriend."

I nod, slowly. "I do. And... and... I don't care if I fail or if I never graduate. I'm not coming back here. I'm gonna do those science tests at home this weekend and be done with this."

He considers this for a moment. His lips purse a little and his eyes briefly fall to the floor, then recover and find mine again. "You should've said no if you didn't want to."

"I shouldn't have had to say no. You're a fucking teacher."

"I'm not really a teacher, Shannon. I'm a private contractor. And you never said no."

"I never said yes."

"You think I raped you?"

"No," I say, swallowing. I don't really think that. I'm pretty sure girls who come like that aren't getting raped. But this guy has bad written all over him. "You've been watching me? How long? A month, you said? You didn't even know me until yesterday. So just what the fuck?"

He rubs his scratchy beard and I have to close my eyes as I imagine how that felt nestled between my legs. "You need a day to process? Fine. But you better be here tomorrow."

He turns to leave, but I stop him with, "Or what?"

He doesn't turn back. Just lets the door close in his absence.

I stay in the bathroom for a few more minutes, trying to plan my escape from the building. But it's dumb. Mateo is gone. Probably walked straight out of the building.

And he lied. There *are* people here. A janitor, one class still going. A lady in the office. Jesus Christ. Did any of them hear me? See us?

I feel a little pool of wetness between my legs at that thought.

Outside it's cool and dark, but only because it's January. I hate the weather here in Southern California. Hate it. I can't even explain how three hundred and sixty days of sunshine pisses me off. And that rain yesterday just fucked with my head. Made me homesick or something.

Sunday. He was a good find though.

Mateo. He was... well, a good fuck, for sure.

I spot Sunday's black Acura and walk out into the parking lot to meet him. It's only then that I realize Mateo is sitting in a white Mustang with double blue racing stripes running down the hood a few rows away. He's fucking watching me.

And who drives a car like that? I mean, come on.

Sunday pulls up and I hurry to the door, pulling it open, slipping inside, and slamming it shut as fast as I can. I want to scream, *Drive!* But I take a breath and when he looks over and says, "Hey," I force myself to relax.

"Hey."

"Everything OK?"

"Yeah. Just tired, you know."

He nods and looks down at the steering wheel. "Yeah, about that. Do you need somewhere to stay tonight?"

"Um." Fuck. I haven't even had time to think about Jason. "No," I finally decide. "I should go home. Patch things up."

"You sure? Because you can stay at Phil's. I won't even bother you there."

"No, really. I'm fine. I need to sort shit out. And I haven't seen my niece in two days. I have to go home and make sure things are…"

"Things are what?"

I was gonna say OK. But then I realize what that implies about Jason's parenting skills. He's an asshole. I hate his guts. But I've never seen him be anything but loving towards Olivia, so it's not fair to give strangers the impression that he's not taking care of her.

"Just cool. You know."

"OK," Sunday says, pulling away from school. I glance at Mateo as we drive by and he stares back, but what's on his mind escapes me. Because he's got his no-expression expression on.

Sunday talks about his day as we drive home. It's not a long drive, and I do my best to look interested, but holy shit. I just fucked a teacher on a classroom desk. My shirt is wet with his fucking come. And Sunday is acting like we've been BFF's for decades instead of hours.

"You can pull in the alley," I tell him, once we get over to the intersection of Broadway and West. "I live at the very end."

We have the only apartment with a back patio. It's dark, and cool, and flanked by tall bushes that partially hide the 5 freeway twenty feet down an embankment. It's almost like living next to a river with the sound and the wind of the cars whizzing by. I love the patio, and how we got lucky with this apartment, I have no idea. We have two parking spots. The garage and the space that leads up to our patio. There's a nice tall wooden gate that gives us privacy from the alley, and the patio leads to a glass slider in the living room. It's pretty much the only thing this apartment has going for it.

"So," Sunday says, the car idling in the empty space in front of the patio. "I'll be right here at seven-thirty."

I stop thinking for a moment and just enjoy him. His broad shoulders, his handsome face, his nice smile. He's hot, for sure. But I enjoy him for more than the way he looks. Lots of guys are handsome. Mateo, for instance, is fuck hot. But Sunday is… interested. In me, I think. Or maybe I'm just making it all up. But he seems interested.

"OK," I say back. "Thank you."

"Anytime, Daydreams." And then he winks and grins the grin of a boy who likes a girl.

I close the door and smile at him as he backs out of the parking space and turns the car around, my insides fluttering in a totally different way than they did back at school with Mateo.

Have I ever felt this before? I ask myself.

Felt what?

Normal.

10

Inside the apartment Jason is sleeping on the couch and Olivia is in that little baby swing she loves. She's wide awake with the remnants of milk on her lips, staring up at me with her big blues, content to listen to the news blaring from the TV.

"Hey, Olivia," I whisper as I get her out and hold her close. "Missed you."

"Miss me too?" Jason asks.

I turn and glare at him, but keep my mouth shut as I take Olivia to the kitchen, run the hot water, and then wipe her face with the washcloth he uses to bathe her. She coos at me and even though I really hate her father, I love her a lot. She looks like Jill's baby photos. My sister might've been a loser, but she was beautiful and I hate her for leaving me, for leaving *us*, and for all the things she will miss because she was stupid.

"I'm sorry, OK?"

I say nothing. I have nothing to say.

That's not true. I have an entire Wikipedia filled with things I want to say. Things I want to scream at the world. But it's locked up tight and I'm sure as shit not letting it out in front of Jason.

Jason walks up behind me and takes Olivia out of my arms. She coos at him too. And why not? He's her father. She loves him.

That hurts me for some reason.

Jason grabs my chin, but it's not in a mean way. He turns my head to make me acknowledge him. "I'm sorry," he repeats, looking for evidence of his fist on my face. I looked earlier and it's hardly even a bruise. It's mostly yellow and will probably fade in a day or two.

I look up at Jason and find some semblance of sincerity in those blue eyes of his. I should say sorry as well. That's what people do during an apology. But I have nothing to be sorry for, so I'm not gonna say it.

"You can stay here as long as you want, Shan. But I could use some help with Olivia."

I nod. "Sure."

"I got a job at night. So if you could just watch her when I go out, I'd appreciate it."

"OK."

He holds Olivia out to me and I take her back, pressing her close to my chest in a hug I need more than she does. "She ate about an hour ago."

"What kind of job did you get?"

"Nothing special." He walks off down the hall to the bedroom he shares with the baby.

Jason is a chef at a hotel near Disneyland. He works breakfast and lunch shift now, so I assume he's picked up another shift at another restaurant. In San Diego he was a hotshot at a locally famous restaurant on the beach in La Jolla. He was probably considered well-off down there. But I've heard him complain enough about the daycare bill for

Olivia to know that's not the case now. Kids are fucking expensive.

When we first moved here I thought it was so he could be near his family. But then he said we were never going to see them. So that sorta sucked. It might've been nice to add a few real grown-ups to my life.

I take the baby back to the living room and put her back in the swing.

"Can you do laundry tonight?" Jason asks, walking out from the hallway and grabbing his keys from the small table next to the kitchen. "She's out of t-shirts."

"Sure," I say, glancing down at my own soiled t-shirt.

"Be back late," he says. He leaves through the front door and walks by through the kitchen window as he makes his way to the alley where he's parked.

I change my clothes and put on shorts and a tank top, then start the laundry. Olivia is asleep in her swing when I come back from loading the washer, and I grab my backpack and pull out the book we were issued in English class today. I try to do all my homework in class because I'm not a homework-at-home kind of girl. But my assignment for English is reading *The Good Earth*, and I sorta got hooked on it in class. That teacher makes us read aloud in class. Twelfth fucking grade and we're reading aloud. I paid no attention to what they were reading and I'm about halfway.

But this school, you know? It's not the best. It's definitely near the bottom as far as performance goes. And I think that teacher knows that most of those kids will never pick up a book outside of school and this is the only way to get them to read.

I think I can finish this book tonight and have that report written tomorrow in class, so English is a non-issue for the next couple weeks.

My phone buzzes in my backpack, so I reach over and look at the message.

Unknown number: I'm at your door.

I look up at the front door, but then a knock on the slider to my right makes me jump. Mateo is standing on the back patio.

"What the fuck?"

"Let me in," he says. I can't hear him so much as read his lips.

"No, get out of here." I glance over at Olivia to make sure he didn't wake her.

"Then come outside."

The door isn't locked, I know that for sure. So he could come in if he wanted to. But he doesn't. He waits.

"Shannon," he says. "Come. Out. Side."

I get up and walk over to the slider. His eyes track up and down my body, taking in my bare legs and shoulders. "What do you want?"

"Just to talk," he says.

I open the slider a few inches. "I don't want to talk, Mateo." As soon as I say his name, he smiles and Jesus Christ, that flutter is back. I actually get wet for his smile. "I'm busy watching my niece," I say, trying to cover my reaction.

"I need to know if you wanted it or not."

"What?"

"Did you want it, Shannon? Because if you didn't, I'm fucking sorry, OK?"

I stare at him. He's got no jacket on even though it's chilly out, and I can see all his tattoos in the light that filters through the bushes alongside the freeway. He's very tall and I'm not, but I'm standing on the ledge of the slider, so I'm about up to his chin right now. He leans forward, pressing his hands on either side of the glass and doorjamb, so that I'm between his arms. I can't help but look at the shadows that form on the curve of his muscles.

I have no clue what to say. Yes, I wanted it. I'd do it again if he made another move. But I don't want to tell him that. I feel like he's pulling me into something that feels good in all the wrong ways.

"Can I come inside?"

"My brother-in-law—"

"Is out. I just watched him go."

"He'll be back though."

"When?" Mateo's eyes drop to my breasts, which are responding much like the wetness pooling between my legs. A few seconds later and I'm throbbing for him. What the fuck is wrong with me? "*When*, Shannon?"

"Why?"

"Because I think I gave you the wrong impression back at school."

"What impression did you give me?"

"You tell me."

"Look—"

He reaches out and touches my peaked nipple. He pinches it, rolls it between his fingers. And even though I know I should stop him or slap his face, I am still.

"You like it," he says, not a question. "Just admit it. You like it." And then his whole hand grabs my breast and he squeezes, but not hard. A slow, kneading squeeze that ignites the desire inside me.

"Why are you doing this?"

"Why aren't you stopping me? Hmm?" he asks, just before he leans in and kisses me on the mouth. It's different this time. It's soft and slow. His lips aren't as hard and pressing. His tongue slips inside me and we tangle together. His hand wraps around my head, urging me to kiss him deeper. And just as I start to get into it, he pulls back. "Is he really your boyfriend?"

"What?" I swallow, looking into his green eyes.

"That guy who picked you up. Is he really your boyfriend? Because I've seen you with him before."

"Why are you watching me?"

"Answer my question first."

"No. Just friends," I say, my heart beating faster. "So far," I add.

Mateo stares into my eyes for a few moments of silence. "You're going to stay just friends, understand?"

"What if I don't want to be just friends with him?"

"Then I won't fuck you again."

"Who says I want you to fuck me again?"

The hand on my breast slides down my stomach, then slips inside my shorts. His fingers find my pussy wet.

"You do."

God, his answer just makes me wetter.

"But before we do it again, I need a yes. I know what we're doing is wrong, Shannon."

I gulp air. "Then why are you here? Why are you doing this?"

"Tell me to go and I will."

"You're not listening. That's not what I'm asking. I just want to know why."

He takes his hand out of my shorts and backs up one step.

"You've been watching me?"

He just stares at me, like he's having some deep internal battle.

"OK," I say, grabbing the handle on the slider and starting to push it closed. But he covers my hand and stops it.

"I live across the street."

"What?"

He inhales deeply and throws up his hands. "I live across the street. Across Broadway." He nods his head towards the alley. "I've seen you in Bill's. You eat there all the time."

"Oh." It's far less creepy than I'd been imagining. Sort of anticlimactic, actually. "Well, I've had my share of stalkers, thank you. It's not a turn-on for me."

He smiles, but looks away, like he's trying to hide it.

"What?"

"How many stalkers?" he says, giving me a sideways glance.

"One serious one."

"Define serious," he says, his smile fading.

"I had to go to court and get a restraining order."

"When was this?"

"When I was thirteen."

"Thirteen? Jesus Christ."

I shrug. "I started early. Got a little wild. Paid the price and learned my lesson."

"He scared you?"

I take a deep breath and nod. "Very much."

"Where is he now?"

"Thousands of miles away. It's not a big deal, but I like to be in control. I don't think that's too much to ask."

"Control of what?"

"Life," I sneer.

"You can't control life, Shannon."

"I can control whether or not I get fucked in a school."

"So you wanted me to stop?"

"That's not what I'm saying—"

"Then what are you saying? Because I'm confused."

"Me too."

"Do you want to date that guy who picked you up?"

"What if I do?"

"I don't ever take second place. So let me know now and I'll leave."

I weigh my options for a moment. I believe him. I really do think he'll leave. And I think tomorrow he'll either quit the teacher gig with some excuse, or just be professional from now on. So this is my chance to set a limit.

"Shannon? Do you want to date him?"

I shake my head. "He's just a friend right now. But I like him. He's nice."

"I'm not nice."

"Is that a statement or a question?"

"Both."

"Well, why the fuck would I give up a nice guy for you?"

"Because you like the thought of me more."

"You sure do presume a lot for not knowing anything about me."

"You just said you were wild. You let me fuck you in the classroom. You came. You're wet. I know enough."

"Yesterday you made some snide remark about not knowing what's good for me. I'm failing to see anything about you that's good for me."

"You came," he repeats. "That was good for you."

"You want to fuck me and I can get in trouble for that. So how is *that* good for me?"

"I'm the one taking the risk, Shannon. You're eighteen, you're allowed to sleep with whoever you want. I'm the teacher so I'm the one who will lose my job."

"So why do this?"

"I don't give a fuck about the job. I give a fuck about you. Tell me what you want. Do you want me to quit if we continue? Because I'll find you another teacher."

"But why me?" I just don't get it.

"Why not you? Why are you so insecure? I like the way you look. I like the way you bite your lip when you're choosing food from Bill's. I like that angsty expression on your face all the time. The one that says I've got problems, leave me the fuck alone. I like this." And then he leans in and kisses me, his hands in my hair before I even realize what's happening.

But I kiss him back. Again.

He moans into my mouth. "I like your hair. I like your eyes. I like your legs, and your pussy, and your tits. I wanted to fuck you the minute I saw you. And I was gonna tell Bowman no until I watched you about to lose your shit in the office yesterday morning. So I said yes. And now I want you to say yes too."

He waits for half a second and when I say nothing, he starts kissing me on my neck. "Say yes," he whispers. I get a chill down my spine and that tingly feeling is back. "Say yes, Shannon. Because I'm not going to keep going until you say no. We're not having the rape conversation again."

He kisses me on the lips, gentle this time, our connection longer, our tongues slower. My hands come up to his neck, something I do when I'm getting turned on. But he pulls me outside, grabs my wrists, and pushes me up against the stucco wall.

I stare up at him feeling a little helpless, but at the same time, I know I can stop him with one word.

Make him continue with one word as well. It's my choice.

"Yes." I say it before I change my mind. I know this is a bad idea. Everything about him is a bright red flag for me. But I said it, and his hands are already back where I want them. Squeezing my breast and slipping into my shorts. He fingers me, little flicks across my clit. It sends intense sensations through my body.

"Take your clothes off."

"What?"

"I don't want to repeat everything, Shannon. And I don't want to explain everything. Just fucking do it."

I look towards the alley.

"No one can see. There's a seven-foot-tall gate."

I look the other direction. There's another patio just fifteen feet away.

"No one can see you there, either. This is a very private patio. Consider it your initiation."

"Init—"

"Stop talking," he says with a finger over my lips. "And take your fucking clothes off." He growls that last part and my heart thumps. His fingertips play with the hem of my shirt, tickling my belly. "Off."

I stare him in the eyes as I reach down and grab my tank top and begin lifting it over my head. He steps back a few paces, like he needs to get a better look at me. I hold the small bit of fabric in my hand and wait.

He smiles and takes my shirt, stuffing it in his back pocket. "Now those." He points to my shorts. I glance inside real quick to check on Olivia.

"She's sleeping. I can see her from here. Off."

I take a few deep breaths. What the fuck am I doing? But I'm already unbuttoning my shorts. I pull the zipper down, look up at Mateo—he's smiling—and then wiggle them over my hips and let them fall to the ground at my feet.

"Are you afraid?"

"Should I be?" I whisper back in a small voice that comes off as very much afraid.

"You tell me, Shannon. My opinion doesn't matter."

I hook my thumbs into the elastic of my panties and let them drop to the ground as well. When I look up at Mateo, he's like a wolf. Like he wants to eat me alive.

"Should I leave you like this?"

"What?"

"Are you wet?"

I let out a long breath and nod.

"Show me."

Jesus. This man. He's not gonna be easy. He's gonna make me work for everything.

"Show me," he says again, only this time with more force.

I reach down between my legs and play with myself, gathering the wetness on the tips of my fingers. I hold them up and they glisten in the light filtering through from the freeway.

He steps forward again, closing the distance between us, takes my fingers in his hand and places them in his mouth.

I have to close my eyes. My knees get a little weak and I'm eternally grateful that this stucco wall is holding me up.

"I'll see you tomorrow, Shannon."

"What?" I gasp.

But he's already turned away. "Mateo," I whisper-yell. "Mateo."

"Stay away from Danny Alexander, Shannon. He's bad news."

And then Mateo pushes the gate open and walks through.

"Who the fuck is Danny Alexander?" I ask myself.

12

I figure it out, of course. Sunday is Danny Alexander. I just didn't know his last name.

A second later I get a text.

Unknown Number: I mean it. Stay away from him. Walk to school tomorrow.

Shannon: Who is this?

Unknown Number: Funny girl. I'll make you pay for that tomorrow in class.

Shannon: I think I owe you one, actually. So I'll take that ride and let him know I don't need any more on the way. I'm not going to drop a friend for a guy like you.

Unknown Number: What kind of guy am I?

Shannon: The kind who gets me wet and leaves me hanging.

My phone rings and I almost drop it. "Hello?"

"Rub one out while I'm on the phone then."

"What?"

"Shannon, I'm serious about saying things twice. I hate it. Don't ask me for clarification when you heard me perfectly well."

"I'm not—"

"You are. Now go into your bedroom, lie down on your futon, and play with yourself until you come."

I just stand there.

"Let me know when you're in bed."

I let out a frustrated exhale, but I walk to my room, slip inside, and lie down.

"Turn on the light."

"Why?"

"So I can watch."

I look up at my patio-facing window and there he is. I can barely make him out in the darkness, but I see him well enough.

"Do it," he says. "You might like to think you're in control, but you're not. I am."

"You're creepy, Mateo."

"Thank you. But you're keeping me waiting."

"I told you, I don't like stalkers."

"I'm not a stalker. I'm your boyfriend."

How many times can he stun me silent in one day?

I get up and flip the light on, walk back to my futon, and lie down. But instead of lying down the right way, so my feet face the opposite wall, I lie down sideways, so Mateo can watch.

I'm sick. I realize this.

But I'm turned on like crazy too. So I close my eyes and reach between my legs.

"Fuck, you're hot," he says into the phone. "Stick your fingers inside yourself."

I gush at that. Like, I'm so fucking wet, I might have a problem.

Mateo starts breathing harder on the other end of the phone. "Are you getting off?" I ask.

"Shh," he says back. But I know he is. I picture him in my head. His fat cock in his fist as he pumps up and down along his shaft. I picture myself lying on the desk in the classroom, panting with surprise and lust. I picture the look on his face when he came on my shirt.

I come with that picture in my head. We groan at the same time, him in the phone next to my ear.

"Feel better?"

I nod.

"Lick your fingers."

God, I want to come again. Like right now. But I do as he says and place them in my mouth.

"What do they taste like?"

"You," I say softly. "They taste like you."

I don't even bother looking up at the window. I can almost feel his smile. "You're perfect," he whispers back. "Should we make it even?"

"Wha—How?"

"I'll let you watch me get off tomorrow in class. Don't be late."

And then I get the hang-up beeps. I stare at the phone for several seconds, relaxing into my post-orgasm state, lying naked in my bed, and thinking about all that happened today. This man, I moan internally. He's probably more than I can handle. No, not probably. He is. Ten years makes a big difference in sexual appetite.

I have no idea what all that was but holy hell, it was hot. And I like it. I might not think it's normal, but I like it. And I'm going to picture his perfect cock and what he might look like sitting in that chair at school when he beats off in front of me.

Sick, Shannon. You're sick.

But I don't care.

I get up and grab my shorts from the patio, realizing that he took my shirt with him.

What will he do with it? Smell it as he jerks off? Wrap it around his cock? Sleep with it under his pillow?

I smile at that image and walk back inside to put my clothes back on. I check on Olivia. She's still asleep, so I go back to reading my assignment for English, wondering what kinky shit Mateo will have for me tomorrow.

Another text comes in. It's a picture of a fully erect cock from Unknown Number shooting semen all over my tank top.

He fucking came on my shirt and sent me a picture of it.

Unknown Number: Tomorrow it will be your face. But don't worry, I'll have my fingers inside you when I do it. You can come on them.

I go back in my room and lie on the bed.

Facing the window.

It takes me less than thirty seconds to come again.

"Why not?"

I sigh. Poor Sunday. He's confused. "I got back with my ex-boyfriend," I lie. "And he doesn't want me riding to school with anyone."

"OK." Sunday sighs as we turn into the parking lot. "But you know what they say. Once an ex, always an ex."

"Do they say that?" I laugh.

He smiles big but doesn't look at me as he pulls into a parking spot. "They do, Daydreams. They absolutely do. So when the shit goes bad again, you know where I am."

"You'll be here, huh?"

"I will," he says.

We both get out of the car and then we're standing on opposite sides of the hood again. "See you at lunch? Surely he doesn't care if you sit with friends at lunch?" Sunday asks.

"Yup, see you at lunch."

He smiles as he turns away and just like yesterday, a couple of other boys join in with him as they walk.

I turn away too, heading to my locker out in no-man's-land.

"Hey, Daydreams," I hear from behind me. I turn to see Sunday smiling at me. "Don't ditch me, OK? I still like you."

"Promise," I say. I watch him turn back to his friends and they push him and probably make jokes about him saying that in front of everyone. But I like that about him, I realize. He's honest. And even though Mateo said to stay away, I really don't understand what makes Sunday such a bad guy. It's not like he's a teacher fucking a student, right?

First period is graphic design, which is pretty much the only class I enjoy. But since I took nothing but art most of last year, it's not challenging.

I daydream instead of working today. First Sunday, since he's fresh in my mind. But Mateo too. I have no idea what to expect at class this afternoon. I don't have that stupid science class beforehand, so I don't need to be there until five. I guess that gives me time to figure out a ride since I can't rely on Sunday anymore.

Fowler shows up for second period with no apology for missing yesterday. Maybe I'm just sheltered, but if a teacher didn't show up for class in Ohio, I'm pretty sure they'd be fired.

California is a mystery to me. Everyone is so different.

I walk laps with Josie and Mary, listening to them chat about boys, as usual. But I don't add anything. Every girl I come into contact with is only interested in prom. I'm definitely not going to prom. Not that I even have a date because I'm pretty sure Mateo has no plans to take me. Not that he could. Older men definitely have their limitations.

Economics is boring. And then it's lunch. I wander over to the wall where Sunday and his friends sit and I come in on the middle of a conversation about me.

"What?" I ask Rocky.

"I was just telling them how you went off on the counselors the other day."

"Jesus, that's old news, guys. And way less interesting than it sounds."

"You're just a tough chick, Shannon," Rocky says.

She goes on and on about it for several more minutes and when she gets to the end, I realize Sunday never told her about my almost-breakdown. I look over at him and he's smirking, a crooked smile that lights up his dark eyes. "Wanna ham sandwich?" he asks me, holding one out. "They're the only edible thing on the menu."

I take it. "Thanks." I'm starving. He looks pleased as I eat in silence, just listening to the chatter of his friends.

But he never brings up our conversation or the fact that I said I won't take rides from him anymore. I'm impressed with that, actually. Most guys would be all, *Fuck you, bitch.* You know? I've had my share of boyfriends. I've had my share of choices too. And no matter who you choose, there is always someone unhappy with you about it.

But he's not unhappy. Or if he is, he hides it very well. He takes it all in stride. Like he's got some secret. Something in his back pocket that will change my mind. Like all he has to do is bide his time.

And it's a smart move. Because I do like him. And how practical is Mateo as a real boyfriend? What could we possibly have in common?

Sex.

I almost blush when the word manifests in my mind.

I don't know why he makes me so turned on, but just thinking of him right now is enough to make me want it.

"Why are you blushing?"

I look up from my thoughts and realize everyone is getting up to go to their next class. "Um…" I laugh.

"You're thinking about me, huh?"

"A little bit," I confess. "I'm curious about why you're so nice to me, actually."

Sunday grabs my backpack and motions for me to walk with him.

I do. He's got my pack, right?

"I'm nice to everyone I like."

"Oh." I chuckle a little under my breath.

"You're pretty," he says, shooting me a sideways look. "And smart. AP classes. I got a lot of details about you when we were sitting in the counseling office."

"Yeah, that kinda sucks. No privacy."

"Well," he says, veering off into the main building where my English class is next period. "You handled it well. Aside from the three fucks."

I laugh out loud at that one. "Bowman should've suspended me. I was expecting it, actually."

"He didn't because he likes you too."

"Right."

"Nah, really. I watched him when you were talking about your geometry class. He was fascinated. Like you're his dream student and he can shove you into being a productive adult if he can just get you through second semester senior year."

"He's nosy. He read my file. He knows about my sister. My situation."

"What is your situation?" We stop outside my classroom and Sunday leans on a locker. And for some reason I don't get the feeling that he's being nosy.

"My sister died right after she gave birth to my niece. I live with my brother-in-law and the baby right now."

"He's the one who hit you." It's not a question.

"I got him back, so don't worry about me. Sometimes you just need to have a who's-in-charge fight, ya know?"

He stares at me. His smile is gone. "No, Shannon. I don't know. I've had my share of fist fights, but I've never had them with the people I live with."

"You're lucky, I guess."

"I guess I am."

I don't know what to say after that, so I just look down at my Chucks.

"I'll take you to school if you want. I mean, after-school school."

I should say yes. Everything inside of me wants to say yes. But it's not fair to him. "Nah, my brother-in-law is gonna take me. Make up for the other night. And buy me dinner," I add, to sweeten the story.

Sunday hands my pack over and I take it. "OK," he says. "I'll see you tomorrow at lunch then."

"Yeah, lunch is my new favorite."

He shoots me one of those amazing smiles, and with something that looks a little bit like reluctance, walks off.

The rest of my day goes by fast. You know how it goes—you don't have a ride to night school and you're wishing the day could be longer so you can figure it out. But no. Two-thirty comes way too fast and after I go to my locker and get what I need for tonight, I have to face the fact that it's the bus or it's walking.

And I can't stand at the bus stop in front of school, because Sunday hangs out at the arcade across the street.

So I walk home and sit on the couch until four when I have to decide.

What if I don't go? Will Mateo come here looking for me?

I don't want that. I was lucky Jason didn't come home and find us out on the patio last night. I really don't need any more drama.

So I walk back up to Lincoln and catch the bus a few blocks down from school.

I hate my life the whole twenty-minute ride down to Gilbert. I should not have to take the bus to night school. I should not even have to go to night school. Everything is unfair.

I tuck my pity party away when I get to school, but when I pull on the door to go inside, it's locked.

I look around for Mateo's car or bike, but the lot is empty.

I will cut a bitch if I just hauled myself over here for no reason. I swear to God, I will—

The loud roar of a bike cuts me off and even though I don't want to feel the wetness between my legs, there it is.

I throb for him.

He pulls up next to me and pulls a helmet out of one of his side packs. "Get on," he says, revving the engine.

"Where are we going?"

He ignores me. Stares straight ahead.

"Fucking fine," I sigh. I push the helmet onto my head, swing my legs over the seat, and scoot up next to his back.

Throb for him.

"Scoot closer," he says over his shoulder.

I can feel the muscles in his back through his t-shirt

because he has no jacket on. It was hot today and typically I'd be bitching about eighty-degree weather in January. But those muscles under his shirt change my mind. I press my head into his back and smell him as we take off.

We end up at his house, which is indeed less than two hundred yards from my own apartment. I take off the helmet and hand it over to his waiting hands, watching as he tucks it back into the packs. "Why didn't you just text me and tell me to come here? I took the bus over to Gilbert."

He looks at me with something that might be curiosity. "To see how you'd manage to get to school without your friend's ride."

"Asshole. You could've saved me an hour of time."

"Bygones, Shannon."

I screw up my face at him. "What?"

"Just let it go. You're here now."

Here is a small bungalow, typical of old-town Anaheim. One story, possibly an attic, with those thick columns on either side of the front porch. We're not in front, which is good. I don't need any nosy neighbors seeing me here with him. We're in the back where he's got a huge five-car garage.

I'm not kidding, five cars. That garage has to be twice the size of the house. "What's with the massive garage?" I ask.

"Cars," he says.

OK, asshole. Remind me again why I'm with him and not Sunday?

I follow him up the back steps and he holds the door open for me, waving me forward.

He grabs my ass and squeezes hard as I walk past.

I throb. And gasp. But mostly throb.

That's why, Shannon. He's gonna fuck me. But then... "Hey, you said I could watch you jerk off in the classroom."

That makes him smile. I like the smile. He likes me dirty, I realize. Dirty makes him smile. "We can do that tomorrow when you have to go for science. But until you finish all those tests you spoke so highly of at our first meeting, we meet here at three o'clock on Mondays, Wednesdays, and Fridays. And if you're a bad girl, Saturdays and Sundays too."

"I can't on Saturdays. I told my brother-in-law I'd babysit for him while he works during the day."

"Ah," he says, turning to the fridge to grab two beers. "Well, we better make the most of the days we have then, right?" He hands me a beer and I take it. "But don't think we won't be fucking in the classroom too."

"Is that the only thing you want from me?" It comes out with a sneer.

"Nope," he says, popping the top of his beer off using the counter. He takes mine, does the same, and hands it back. "But it's definitely up there at number one."

"Why? You like the idea of getting caught?"

"No, Shannon, I like the *possibility* of getting caught. Fucking you here will be wild and fun. But fucking you there will be erotic. Taboo. Do you like taboo sex?"

"I'm not really sure what that means." I laugh, taking a drink of my beer to hide my blush.

He lifts me up and sets me on the counter, spreading my legs and moving in between them. "Forbidden relationships, Shannon. Like this one."

"Hmm, but it's not really all that dangerous for me, though. That's what you said last night."

"Who cares? You're not even into it yet. I am. So I'm the one who needs the thrill."

Jesus. I am not used to twenty-eight-year-old guys. They just say whatever the fuck they want. I'm used to Sundays. Although he's sweeter than I'm used to as well.

"You better be thinking about me," Mateo says. His hands are on my thighs, rubbing them softly.

I'm definitely thinking about him.

"And don't worry. If sucking my dick in the classroom isn't enough to thrill you, I'll think up something that will."

My mouth makes this little O shape. I exhale as I picture me on my knees in front of his chair in the classroom, my lips wrapped around his thick cock.

"That do it for you?"

I nod. I cannot wait.

"Well, good." And then he turns around, grabs a red book off the table, and plops it down on the counter next to me.

"What's that?"

"Your homework. You like tests? You want to pass this class with tests? I got your book changed. They use this one for the self-paced trig class at Fullerton College. So it will transfer."

I shake my head a little. The switch from sucking him off in the classroom to trig throws me back.

"What?" he asks, a smile creeping out. "You thought I was gonna pass you for sucking my cock? Please. You gotta earn everything with me, Shannon."

"OK, I'm just surprised by the subject change." But what else is new. Everything about him is a surprise.

"So here's the deal. You do one test each time we're together and then I fuck your brains out."

"Hand it over." I laugh.

"Ah, but there's a catch. You gotta pass the test too."

"Dammit. I can't just pass a test in trig."

"They typically only have a few questions."

"Yeah, but those questions will take forever to work out."

"Well, since you're a beginner, I'll cut you some slack for the first week. Every time you take a test, I'll let you suck my dick."

"Oh, my God." He's crazy.

"If you get one question right, I'll lick your pussy." He whispers that last part in my ear and I'm really going to need new underwear.

I take a deep breath. "What if I get two right?"

"Nah, it's not that easy, grasshopper. Every time we meet and you take a test, you suck my dick. Every time you get one right, I lick your pussy. If you don't pass the test, you don't get fucked. But maybe I'll let you rub one out in front of me to hold you over until next time."

I throb. I need that cock. I mean, if I didn't have to be so close to him, I could do without. But I will die if I have to come here for weeks and not get laid.

"And just to make it interesting, you're gonna study naked. Take off your clothes."

I don't know much about this world. I'm only eighteen. I feel like a little baby seahorse in a sea of sharks, that's how confusing life is for me right now. But I do know one thing for sure.

I should walk out of this house, call the police, and tell them what Mateo is doing.

I also know I'm not even close to doing those things. Some fucked-up part of me is intrigued, turned on, and on my way to being addicted to him.

I don't give him the *WTF are you talking about* look or act shocked. Why would I? He prepped me for this, I realize. Last night when he came over.

'Take your clothes off' is a command I've heard before. Something I've obeyed before. He even gives me these few seconds to work this all out.

And it pays off. Because I lift my shirt over my head, slip my jeans down my legs, unclasp my bra, let it slide down my arms to the floor, and then wiggle out of my underwear. I stand there naked in front of him as a condition of being given the opportunity to learn trig, take a test, give him a blow job, get at least one question right, and get my pussy licked.

I'm officially sick.

But instead of thinking about how many therapy sessions I will require when this semester is over, I wonder... "How hard can the first test be?"

Mateo actually laughs.

I love laughing Mateo.

"You're gonna pass that one, Shannon, but it won't be as easy as you think," he says, taking in my body with that wolfish gaze he has. "So let's get started." He points to the small kitchen table. There are only two chairs, one on each side of a window that faces the driveway. The blinds are up and the curtains are open. The house is sitting up higher than the driveway so if anyone did walk by, they probably could not see me.

"A kid from your high school lives next door," Mateo says, probably reading my mind. Because that's when I see the window across the driveway. There's no blinds or curtains in that one either. "If you sit here too long," Mateo says, flipping on the lights—I look up at the bulbs dangling over the table—"it will get dark out, and believe me, he *will* see you. And he'll see me, my hands fisting your hair, as I fuck your face."

I look over at him. I want to ask all the questions. Like why? Why do you do this shit?

But I know why. It's the same reason I let him drag me into this completely insane scenario. He likes it. It turns him on to think of people watching us. It turns him on to scare me into doing the things he wants with the threat of humiliation.

So why bother asking? I like it too. I just nod. "We better get busy then."

He bares his teeth in a grin. "I hope you're a quick learner, Shannon."

"I can be."

He frowns. "Explain. I hate wasting my time."

"I'm not good at math, Mateo. I'm good at memorizing things, so I learn the steps to solve the problems and I repeat them on tests. I'm not good at school, I'm just good at tests. That's how I got through those AP classes. So if you want to waste time teaching me theory, or the reasons why math is the way it is, or force me to understand what I'm doing—then we're never gonna fuck again. I just learn the steps. If you really want to help me graduate, teach me how to work the problems and let me do it my way."

"OK," he says in an uncharacteristically soft voice. "Fair enough. Get out a piece of paper."

I look at the folder he's got set up on the table, open it, and take out a piece of graph paper. He pushes a mechanical pencil over to me and I take it and then look up at him expectantly.

"Every section in every chapter has a purpose, and your homework is to read the chapter, find the purpose of each section, and write it down in one sentence on that piece of paper. That's your cheat sheet."

"It's open-book?"

"No," he says, shaking his head. "Life isn't open-book, Shannon. You just think it is because you can look up anything you want on the internet. Answers are free these days. But it's an illusion. You have to work for the answers. And if you're good at remembering things, then you write down the answers that are meaningful so you can look them up when you need them."

"I'm not taking a test today, am I?"

He shakes his head slowly. "I'm not letting you off easy. You're not gonna get this credit without earning it. And I think you're smart enough to realize that what we do after the test has nothing to do with what we do before it."

"Then why am I naked?"

"I like looking at you. And after you write down the purpose of each section in chapter one, I'm going to fuck you anyway. Because I like fucking you too, and even if I had the kind of self-control it would take to let you get dressed and walk home, keeping you frustrated until tomorrow, I don't want to practice it today."

"You're the weirdest guy I've ever met."

He smiles. I long for the laugh, but I only get the smile. "I'll take that as a compliment. Now get to work."

I read the first section. It's easy, so I find the purpose in less than a minute and start writing it down, being careful to make it succinct, so it has meaning to me later.

Mateo cooks. He's making lasagna because he's got the box of pasta out on the counter with some cans of tomato paste. He starts boiling the water first, and then empties the paste in another pot to make the sauce. I'm intrigued by everything. And he's got his back to me, so I can stare at the muscles under his t-shirt and the tattoos down his arms as he works. They are mostly stars, I realize.

Stars. He's a fucking physicist. Or whatever. Astronomer. So that fits. They might even tell a story.

"I don't hear your pencil moving," Mateo says, never turning around from his tasks.

I go back to work and he continues cooking. What I'm doing is not hard. Chapter one of any math textbook is mostly stuff I already know, with a few specific additions. I'm smart enough to know the difference. I pick out the points that are important and write them down.

"Done?" Mateo asks when I set my pencil aside with a sigh.

I look over at him and get stuck on just how much there is to see. He's got his arms folded across his chest, his head tilted a little. Those cannon biceps are bulging and he's leaning back some, allowing me to see the definition of his abs through his tight t-shirt. He must've shaved this morning, because he has less stubble on his face than yesterday. Just a shadow really. I look down at his bare feet and realize he took his boots off at some point. God, I have no idea why that's sexy, but it is. "Done," I confirm.

"How many sections?" he asks.

"Um." I look down at my paper. "Fifteen."

"OK, that's it for today. I'll see you tomorrow at school."

"What?"

"You were hoping for more?"

I laugh. "Well, you did promise more."

"You want it?"

Jesus Christ. He's got an ego he needs stroked? "I'm sitting here naked. I've been wanting it since my underwear hit the floor."

He just stares at me.

"And I thought you'd at least feed me." Fucking lasagna smells good. I would even consider giving up the sex if he'd let me stay for dinner.

He glances over at the oven, which has a timer that says there's forty-five minutes left. I sigh. Big and long. And then push my chair back and get up.

"Is it wet?"

"What?" He scowls at my question. Asshole. It's not that I don't hear him, it's just he's so fucking inappropriate, I have to constantly ask myself if those words really came out of his mouth. I look down at the chair and to my horror, it is. "Yes," I say back.

He smiles. "If you want it, come get it."

I huff out some air. But after a second of thought, I walk over to him. If I ask a question now, he'll give me that frown again. And then he'll probably go on and on and on about some bullshit lesson I need to learn or blah, blah, blah. All I really want is a connection. Just something to make me feel wanted today.

So I take the hem of his t-shirt in my fingertips and begin to lift it. He prickles with goosebumps and I pause to look up into his eyes and realize he's excited. "Keep going," he says in a low growl.

I press my palms against the flat planes of his stomach and drag the fabric upward. He's a lot taller than me, so when I get to his chest, he reaches down and whips the shirt over his head.

He's got tattoos on his chest. Every kind of star you can imagine, all arranged in patterns. I gently touch one, tracing the faint line that connects it to another, and his skin prickles again. "I like these," I say, looking up into his green eyes.

"I like you," he says.

I blush, and look down to hide my smile.

But his fingers lift my chin back up and he says it again. "I like you. Keep going."

I take a deep breath and slip my fingertips inside the waistband of his jeans. I can feel his cock growing under the denim and my body floods with warmth. I slide them against his tanned skin until I get to the buckle. It jingles as I work it free, and then the brown leather falls to either side of his growing bulge.

His hand slips under my hair and he pulls it aside. I look up at him again, and he nods.

Keep going.

I unbutton his jeans and slide the zipper down, and before I even give myself time to think, I reach in and pull him out. He's fully hard now and I know what he wants. But I get the feeling he doesn't want to have to ask for it. So I bend down and settle on my knees in front of him and look up.

He's got a fistful of my hair now, but he doesn't urge me on. He wants to me initiate everything today.

I open my mouth and kiss his tip, my tongue darting out to lick small swirling patterns around his thick head. His hand in my hair gives the slightest push and I have a feeling he can't help that. He's a disciplined guy, I'm realizing. And if he wants me to initiate, then that small urge is a weakness on his part.

I gain a little confidence and open wider so he can slip inside me an inch or so. I let my tongue explore his tight skin, my hand coming up automatically to wrap around his shaft.

"Fuck, yeah," he moans.

I tighten the seal of my lips and suck him in. This gets me a sigh and a tighter grip on my hair. "Mmmmm," I hum.

His hips respond to that by rocking forward an inch or two, and I have to open wider to accommodate the new girth. I ease forward and allow him to penetrate me another inch. My mouth is small, so there is no way I'm taking him all in, but I want to make him sigh and moan some more. So I start bobbing on his cock, taking him in as far as I can, then withdrawing and letting my tongue caress him as I pull away.

"I don't usually like it so slow, Shannon." I look up at him and find his eyes at half-mast like he's enjoying this. "But you can do it any way you want. It doesn't matter."

I keep my eyes trained on his as I continue pushing forward and drawing back. I do go slow. I like it slow and I'm not in a hurry.

"Touch yourself," he says. It's not harsh and I like that too. Slow and soft Mateo is someone I don't know yet, but I'd like to see more of that part of him.

I reach down between my legs and find the pool of wetness. I'm almost embarrassed by how wet I am for him, and he hasn't even touched me yet.

"I want you to come," he says. "I want you to come with my cock in your mouth and your fingers in your pussy."

I take in a deep breath through my nose and start playing with my clit. Small, slow circles at first. I don't think I can come the way he wants, but I'll do anything he asks right now. I concentrate on his dick—licking it, sucking it, and waiting for that grip on my hair that says I'm doing it right.

"Make yourself come," he reminds me.

I reach down farther and insert a finger inside me, probing deeper and deeper each time I take his cock inside me farther.

He moans.

I gush.

"Fuck," he growls.

I swallow, feeling the tip of his cock in the back of my throat, and this time I get another hand gripping my hair.

"Mmmm," I hum again, only now I'm doing it because I'm turned on and not because I'm satisfying him.

He moves my head now, forward and back, a little harder, a little more forcefully with each pass. I fuck myself with my fingers with more enthusiasm too, unable to stop the momentum we're building.

My hands go to his hips to steady myself and then they are tugging his jeans down farther. I let them drop to his knees and stroke the muscles along the back of his thighs.

"I love that," he says.

My hands slide upward, my mouth still fucking him in long strokes. Saliva pools in my cheeks and then drips out over my lips.

He moans again and thrusts his hips forward.

I almost gag, my hands tighten on the curves of his ass, but he pulls back at just the right moment and long strands of saliva dangle until they drop onto my bare legs.

"Come, Shannon," he whispers.

My hand goes back to my thoroughly wet pussy and I begin to stroke. His cock begins to twitch inside my mouth, and then he pulls all the way out and kneels down in front of me. Kissing me on the mouth.

"I want to come down your throat, but I want you to come at the same time." He kisses me again and my tongue can't get enough of him. We tangle together like that for a few seconds, and then he stands back up, taking my silence and enthusiasm as permission.

I stroke myself, wanting all of this more than I'd like to admit. My head begins to spin, my eyes close, and then he pumps his cock into my mouth like he's really fucking me.

I have never given a blow job like this before. It's so much more than I ever knew was possible. His hands fist my hair so hard my scalp begins to burn, his cock reaching deeper and deeper inside me with each thrust. The saliva drips out of my mouth, my throat makes gurgling sounds and my fingers furiously stroke myself.

I feel the warmth of his come as he shoots it into my mouth and I slip two fingers inside myself just as my pussy contracts and my own come begins to drip down until it tickles my wrist.

"Swallow," he says. "Swallow me, Shannon."

I do. Holy fuck, I want every drop of him. I look up into his eyes and he bites his lip and then throws his head back, pumping one last time.

I fall to my ass and lean back until I'm resting on the floor, gasping, exhausted, and wanting desperately to lie down somewhere comfortable as Mateo kicks off his jeans and boxers and steps away from them.

"I'm gonna stay here on the floor and fall asleep," I say.

He laughs. "We're not done yet. I'm not even close to done yet." He scoops me up into his arms and carries me towards the front door.

"What are you—"

"Shhh," he chastises me. "Be quiet and trust me."

He opens the door to the front porch. It's screened in on all sides and it's just about dusk.

"Mateo—"

"Shannon," he growls. "Quiet. No one can see us."

I find that hard to believe. I can see several people from where we stand. One is across the busy street—some lady doing gardening. The neighbor to the left is out, talking to the high-school kid who must live next door. And there's an older woman a couple houses down with a dog on a leash.

"If you're quiet, they'll never know that I'm fucking you on the front porch, just a few feet away."

"You're crazy," I say.

"Not really," he says. "Just adventurous." He sits down on a leather couch, placing me in his lap so we're facing each other. "Did you have fun inside?"

I nod, still feeling the throbbing from my orgasm. I want more. I am dying for more.

"Put my cock inside you."

I lift up my hips and find his wet tip. I rub it along my clit a few times, burying my head into his neck from the sensations. And then I place him at my entrance and ease down.

"Oh, fuck," I say, as he stretches me wide.

"Fuck me," Mateo says. "Fuck me the way you like it so I know how to do it next time."

I forget about the people all around us. I forget about everything. How old he is, how much more experienced he is, how much trouble I will be in if people find out, what they'll call me. I throw it all away because the only thing I have room for is the way he makes me feel.

I place my hands on his shoulders, gripping his hard muscles, and ease up and down so slowly it makes him grimace.

"Slow, then?" he asks.

I nod into his neck, my teeth nipping at his skin, my hands desperate to bring him closer to me. His finger finds my ass, probing the tight entrance just enough to drive me wild.

"Ohhhh," I moan.

"Shhh," he says. "We can be loud inside, but when we fuck out here, we will be quiet." He whispers that so close to my ear, it vibrates through my whole body. The only part I care about is the promise of more.

I want more.

So I ease down, and up, and down and up. I get a rhythm going, my hips moving forward as I press his cock inside me so I can rub my clit against his shaft. Our breath becomes heavy and mine turns into uncontrollable panting.

"Come," he whispers in my ear. "Come on my dick."

I can't help myself. Even if I wanted to wait, I can't. I lean my head into his neck, my fingernails grip his shoulders so hard he growls, and I bite his ear—moaning, and moaning, and moaning so only he can hear me.

We sit there like that until I can feel his come slipping out of me. "We didn't use a condom," I say.

"We don't need one," he says back. "I found your pills in your room last week."

He doesn't give me any time to question him about that statement, because he says, "Lie on me, Shannon," as he rearranges us so we are lying back along the couch and I'm on top of his chest.

I give off a huge sigh.

"Tired?" he asks, dragging a long strand of my hair up and down my back.

"Relaxed," I say.

And then we go quiet. Our breathing evens out and I listen to his heartbeat get slower and slower and if he wasn't still tickling my back with my own hair, I'd be convinced he was asleep.

"Will you come back here on Friday?" he asks, breaking the silence.

"Do I have a choice?"

"Do you think you don't?"

I do, I realize. I could've walked out at any point today. I could've stopped this before it got started if I wanted to. But I don't want to. "I'll come back."

"We're really not going to fuck again until you pass a test."

"I hope you're a good teacher then. Because I could get used to this side of you."

"What side?"

"The quiet side. I don't get enough quiet in my life."

"Mmmm," he says, but it's more of a question. "Your teenage problems are typical? Or atypical?"

I think about this for a moment. I was going to immediately say atypical, but it's a thoughtful question, so it deserves a thoughtful answer. "My mom died a year and a half ago and my sister Jill got custody of me because I was already seventeen. She wanted to move to California. See the world, take a risk, become new people."

"Did you hate the people you were?" he asks.

"I didn't. But I guess she did."

"Then what happened?"

"We bounced around, Escondido first, then San Diego. We always lived with her boyfriends. But then she got pregnant by Jason, my-brother-in-law who I live with now. And we moved up here with him after the baby was born. But she OD'd the day after we moved in. Left me with him, and him with the baby. Olivia's three months old now."

"I think that counts as atypical."

"Me too," I say, but it comes out filled with sadness.

Mateo drops the strand of hair and just uses his fingers to caress my back. It feels so good, I can't even find a word for it. We sit there in silence for a long time and I wonder if he's thinking about me and my sad situation or something else.

"I don't want to hurt you, Shannon."

"Are you hurting me?"

"Am I?"

I shake my head into his chest. "I—" But I have so much I want to say and no good way to let it out. "You're not hurting me."

More silence. I'd like to ask about him back. Learn a little more, see a little deeper. Why is he so weird? Why does he like young girls? Why me, mostly. But when I open my eyes I see the stars.

"Why stars?" I ask instead.

"Astronomy, remember?"

"You love them?"

"How could anyone not love them? They're filled with the mysteries of the universe. When I was a kid I read this book about a star who came to Earth reincarnated as a dog."

I huff out a laugh. "I know that book. *Dogsbody*."

"Yeah," he says. I can feel the smile in his heartbeat. "And it made me wonder if the stars knew all the answers. Because it really bugged me that I'd grow old and never know those secrets. So even though I am nothing but a good test-taker myself, I taught myself math so I could teach myself science. And I've spent the last twenty fucking years trying to get close to them."

"That's why you put stars all over your body? To be close to them?"

He nods. "Turn around and look up."

I force my satiated body to turn so my back is against his chest. He eases us up a little so we're semi-sitting.

I look up. "Oh, wow," I say. "That's cool." There's a skylight in the porch roof. It's wide and long, almost the entire length.

"My dad made me that skylight when I was eleven. I used to have a hammock out here as a kid and I'd sit in that thing looking up for hours."

"Oh, my God, what time is it? I have to get home and watch the baby for Jason. He got a night job to help with bills."

I try to get up, but Mateo's arms wrap tightly around me. "Wait," he says. "You're missing the best part." He points up to the sky and I squint my eyes, trying to follow his guiding path. "There's a meteor shower up there right now."

"Where?" I strain to look for shooting stars, but I can't see anything.

"Ah, you have to know where to look. And it's not dark enough in the city. One day I'll take you somewhere dark and I'll show you everything." He sits up, me still clinging to him, and stands.

"I'd like that," I say as he walks us inside and deposits me in front of the bathroom.

"Clean up."

I go into the bathroom and wash, thinking about how close I feel to Mateo right now. I met him three days ago. How is that possible?

"Hey," he says, knocking at the door before opening it. "Here's your clothes."

"Thanks," I say, taking them from his hands. He holds on to them for an extra second and my eyes meet his. Something passes between us at that moment. I'm not sure what it is, but it feels... intimate.

And then he lets go and closes the door.

I put my clothes back on and walk back to the kitchen. His lasagna smells awesome, but I have to go before Jason gets pissed. So I gather my book and papers as he watches and then stand there, unsure what to say.

He nods to the backpack over my shoulder. "Memorize everything you wrote down today. There will be a quiz tomorrow." He comes over, wraps an arm around my waist, and pulls me in for a parting kiss. "And stay away from Danny Alexander, Shannon. I mean it."

"I know." I shoot him an annoyed look and walk out the back door.

When I get home, Jason is looking out the front window like he's been waiting for me.

"Hey," I say.

"Fucking finally. I told you to be here by six so I can work."

"You never said six." I stop by little Olivia's swing and bend down, but she's fast asleep. "You asked me to help watch her in the evenings. Fine. But I have night school every day. So I'll come home when I'm done. And if you think I'm giving up my weekends—"

"Giving up?" he sneers. "She's your fucking niece."

"Right. But I'm eighteen, Jason. I'm too young to be her mother. You're her father and I'm sorry you got mixed up with my sister—"

"Watch your fucking mouth." He cuts me off. "You're not going to talk about Jill like that now that she's dead."

"Talk about her?" I scoff. "Who the fuck do you think you are? You think you knew her? Well, you didn't. She took an engagement ring from the last guy too, you know. And the one before that and the one before that. So don't go thinking you're special—"

He's across the apartment and slapping my face before I can even finish my sentence. "Fuck you," he says, grabbing my hair and pulling me towards him. "Fuck you."

"You're gonna regret that," I say, pushing him hard in the chest. He lets go of my hair and turns away. "You're gonna fucking regret that."

"No tears this time? No running off to slut around with Phil's piece-of-shit cousin?"

"You know what, you can find another babysitter. I don't need to stay here and if you think I'm going to let you raise her with that temper, you're wrong."

"What are you going to do about it?" He turns back, eyes blazing. "You just said yourself, I'm her father. You're no one to her. I can walk out of here with her tonight and you'll never see her again."

"Did you ever ask yourself," I say, my voice low and filled with venom, "how many men Jill was sleeping with while she was with you?"

"Liar," he says. "Liar." But he knows it's not a lie. I can see it in his eyes.

"You're not even on the birth certificate because you two weren't married when Olivia was born."

"You little fucking liar."

"So maybe I'm the only family Olivia has. And maybe you're the one who's nobody?"

He turns around, grabs his keys and his jacket, and slams the door behind him as he leaves.

I palm my cheek as I check on Olivia. It stings, but it's nothing like the last blow. I really do need to get out of here. And telling Jason that shit about Jill was not the best way to handle things. What if he starts believing that? What if he never comes home and I am the only one left in this world who cares about Olivia? How the fuck would I take care of an infant?

No, it was definitely not a good idea to plant that thought in his head.

A knock at the slider makes me jump.

Mateo is staring back at me from the other side of the glass. Fuck, I hope he didn't just see that.

"Hey," I say, opening the door. He's holding a brown bag in his hands, looking strangely at me. "What?"

"Dinner," he says. "Did I just hear yelling?"

"Yeah, Jason's a dick. He was mad because apparently he thought I was supposed to be here at six so he can work his night job."

Mateo stares at me for a second, but then he looks over his shoulder at the alley, like he's distracted. "You said you wanted me to feed you, so... I gotta go."

And then he walks through the gate and disappears in the alley. Fucker. What the hell am I doing with that guy anyway? In the heat of the moment it makes sense. I'm horny and I just want someone to pay attention to me. But I don't like feeling this way afterward.

There is a part of me that wants to run back to Ohio and pretend the last year never happened, but there's nowhere to go. I have no family there and my friends aren't in any position to take care of me.

And Olivia. I look down at her sleeping body all snuggled up in blankets in the swing. Jason is an asshole, but he seems to love her. I should've shut up about Jill.

I take a bag of food inside and put it on the counter. There's a note stapled to it, making it look like a delivery receipt. That makes me smile. I tug the piece of paper free from the staple and open it up.

Shannon,

Remind me to tell you why I have take-out containers and know how to make lasagna from scratch.

And stay the fuck away from Danny Alexander. I mean it.

M

Fucker.

But I smile. Even though he creeps me out, he does it in all the right ways. And even though he's a teacher and he's fucking me on the side, he's still putting me first by making me work. And even though he wants me to do that work naked and my reward for success is sex, I can't help but trust him.

I'll probably regret that soon. I usually do.

"Hey, Daydreams!" Sunday calls from across Lincoln Avenue as I wait at the light to cross. He's wearing a Distillers t-shirt and some faded jeans with holes in all the right places. I can see a patch of bare skin on one of his thighs.

I walk across the street smiling big at him and when I get close enough so I don't have to shout over traffic, I say, "I know for a fact you didn't see The Distillers in concert to get that shirt because the last time they toured the US was more than ten years ago."

"Hey." He laughs and beams that dangerous grin at me. Jesus, Danny Alexander is fuck hot. "You caught me. But they stopped here in Anaheim on that last tour and Phil went. I stole it from him."

"Hmm," I say, pretending to think this over as we walk onto campus. "I guess second-hand concert shirts still count as authentic."

"Whew," he says, making a big deal of wiping his brow. "I thought I lost street cred with you for a second."

"Were you waiting for me?"

"How'd you guess?"

"Mmmm, well, usually you park your car and start your little bromance with the boys in the lot. But today you are standing at the corner where I cross the street to school."

"It's that obvious, huh?"

"Pretty obvious, yeah."

"Well, it's Thursday, so I wanted to see if that ex of yours is an ex yet. And if so, maybe we can hang out tomorrow night?"

"Ah," I say. "He's still around. And I'm not going anywhere. I babysit my niece on Friday nights."

"Too bad. I know of a good party."

"Sorry to disappoint you. And I'm not much of a party girl these days anyway. I'd just slow you down."

"I'd slow down for you, Shannon."

I stop to look at him, taking a deep breath as I do it. "Are you hitting on me?"

"Yeah."

"Look, I—"

"Hey." He stops me with hands in the air. "I'm not making a move for real until you say you're ready, so don't worry about that. But I'm gonna wait it out, if that's OK with you. And I'm gonna keep asking. I have staying power, Daydreams." And then he gives me this little salute and turns and walks off.

I stare at his ass for a few seconds before turning in the opposite direction. Damn. Why is it that I have no one interested for a whole month, then on the same day I meet two guys who want to take me for a spin? It's not fair. Why couldn't Danny appear after I was done with night school with Mateo?

Maybe that's what I should do? Just get that work done as fast as possible and put night school behind me? I know I can get that science credit in a couple weeks tops. There's only like twelve tests. I might be able to knock out most of them over the weekend. Then I'd only have trig. There's a

116

lot more of those tests because it's a full year's worth of work. But I could take two a week and be done pretty fast.

I don't know what to do about Mateo. I just don't think I have the power it will take to stop this now. I'm caught in a web, right? The more I struggle against him, the harder he'll try. And the harder he tries, the weaker I'll become.

I can see it coming.

Yeah, I need to just get the fuck out of night school. Then he won't have anything to hold over me and I won't have to see him anymore.

I walk into design class a few seconds after the bell rings and the teacher, Mrs. Sheridan, is handing out laptops from giant plastic tubs.

"Everyone," she says. "Shannon"—she singles me out because I'm late—"get in line and sign out your laptop."

I took a lot of graphic design classes, and this design class is senior level, so we're going to make websites. I'm kind of excited about it as I sign out my laptop and take it back to my desk.

"You will be assigned a site where you can legally download images…" She goes on about all the stuff they're providing for us in class. Each laptop is loaded with Adobe software, and we will be expected to deliver a fully functional personal website one week before the end of the semester.

"You need to come up with a domain name that is not already taken and we will register it for you. Treat this project as a resume…" she goes on.

I'm ten steps ahead of her. I've got Photoshop up and I'm already cruising for images from the stock art site. Personal website… I'll have to think about that. I don't have any idea what I want to do after graduation, so that makes it a lot more difficult to decide who my target audience might be.

I get lost in the project and the period flies by way too fast.

"Nice, Shannon," Mrs. Sheridan says, looking over my shoulder at my notepad after the bell rings. "I can't wait to see what you come up with."

"Thanks," I say, reluctantly packing up my stuff. I secretly hope Fowler is absent in PE so I can skip out for the period and continue working, but no such luck. When I get to the gym, he's standing there with a clipboard just outside the locker room.

"So glad you could join us," Fowler sarcastically says.

"Ditto, Fowler," I say back. He's one to talk. I'm like one minute late. He never showed on Wednesday. My phone buzzes in my pants as I walk to my locker to change into the shorts we are required to wear. I don't have a gym uniform. Fuck that. I have better things to spend my money on than a stupid pair of shorts and a t-shirt from a school I don't give a shit about. So I wear some oversized black cargos and a *P!nk* tank top.

I check the message on my phone before leaving the locker room.

Mateo.

Hey, how did his name get into my phone? Sneaky motherfucker.

Mateo: The last thing I said to you was stay away from Danny Alexander and who are you walking onto campus with this morning?

Shannon: Creep. He came up to me and we had a laugh. Get over it.

Mateo: Shannon, I'm not jealous. I'm worried. He's bad news. So stay away from him.

I sigh and stuff my phone into my pocket. Sunday doesn't seem that bad to me. Of course, I met him a few days ago, so what do I know.

Just then I see Mary and Josie waiting for me at the picnic table. They get up to start our mandatory three laps and I fall in next to them. "Hey," I say. "Do you guys know Danny Alexander?"

They erupt into a fit of laughter.

"What?" I ask. "What's so funny?"

"Everyone knows Danny Alexander," Mary says.

"Mary wants to jump his—"

"Stop!" Mary squeals.

"Oh, my God," I say. "Sorry."

"Why do you want to know?" Josie asks.

"Oh, well, he's..."

"He is not!" Mary squeals again. "He likes you?"

"Maybe?" I shrug. "But I have a boyfriend so I'm not interested."

"Yes, you are," Josie says. "Otherwise you wouldn't be asking us about him."

"True." I laugh. "But I've been hearing some things about him. Is he bad news?"

"Definite bad boy," Josie says.

"But oh, my God. I'd still do him," Mary says.

"Like what kind of bad boy?" I ask. "Wears a leather jacket and has tattoos kind of bad boy? Rides a motorcycle kind of bad boy?" Jesus, I just described Mateo.

"Bad boy like his cousin, Phil Alexander, is the biggest drug dealer in Anaheim."

"Phil?"

"You know him?" Mary asks.

"Yeah, he lives down the street from me. Gets me high every once in a while. He's some old friend of my brother-in-law's."

"I rest my case," Josie says.

"Yeah, but smoking a joint and biggest drug dealer in Anaheim are not the same thing," I say. Phil? I just don't see it. He's so cool to me.

"He does a lot more than smoke a few joints, Shannon. I'd stay away from that place."

"But Danny lives in the garage apartment behind the house."

"I hear they've been trying to bust Phil for years and he always gets off."

"Yeah, there was some big sting operation about six months ago but some fancy lawyer from LA showed up and made the whole department look like fools," Mary says.

"Oh." I sigh. "But is Danny involved?"

"Who knows," Josie says. "He sells joints across the street at the arcade. Why do you think a guy like that hangs out in a nickel arcade? He's not playing Pac-Man."

"Hmmm." He does hang out there. Mark, the owner, is another of Jason's childhood friends. He's smoked me out a few times in the back room. And it is a pretty stupid place. I mean I only go there to get high, so it makes sense that Danny would be selling pot.

Still. "Well, Danny seems nice."

"Oh, he's nice all right. He's even nice to me," Mary says. "And pretty much everyone but you guys pretend I don't exist."

"Aww," I say. "I'm sorry. I know the feeling."

"If I could see him coming, I'd take my chances too," Josie says. "But hell, these glasses are mostly for looks. I can't make out faces unless people are right on top of me."

"He picked up your books that one time, remember?"

"How could I forget," Josie says in a dreamy voice.

"So he *is* nice?" I ask.

"I think he is," Mary says. "I don't care what his cousin does. He's always been nice to me, even back in the second grade when the kids used to steal my crutches. He beat someone up for me. Gave him a black eye and everything."

"Dreamy Danny," I say.

"Dreamy Danny." They both sigh.

Mateo is wrong. I trust these two more than I'd ever trust him. He's got an ulterior motive. He wants to fuck me and he wants Danny to keep his distance so he can continue to do that.

I really need to get that night school work done. I need to get the hell away from Mateo Alesci.

I take the bus to Gilbert and turn in five more tests for science. I'm jumpy, so I just put my head down and work.

"You're flying through them," the teacher, whose name I never got, says. "That's what? Nine? You'll be done next week."

"That's the point, right?"

"I think the point is to learn something."

"Well, I'm not the one who said all I have to do to pass with a C is take the unit tests open-book. Expectations come from the top. Even my dumb eighteen-year-old ass knows that."

"I'm not picking a fight with you, Shannon. You're free to take the C, but you could get an A with just the tiniest bit of effort."

"I shouldn't have to take this stupid class in the first place. Why should I care if I get nothing out of it? It's a waste of time and I'm being forced to give up my afternoons to placate some idiot board member who made that stupid rule about when kids are allowed to take science and math credits."

The whole class is looking at me.

"Forget it," I say, walking back to my desk. I grab my stuff and head out of the class, but the teacher follows me. I try to escape to the bathroom, but he grabs my arm.

"Is something wrong?" he asks.

"Why would something be wrong? I just completed half a semester's worth of work in a week. How is that leading you to believe something is wrong?"

Just then Mateo walks around the corner. He narrows his eyes as he approaches. "Everything OK here?" he asks.

"I was just trying to figure that out myself," science teacher says. "She's having a bad day, I think. I didn't mean to upset you, Shannon. I'm happy you're getting your work done quickly. And I'm sorry you got caught in the red tape." He shrugs, looks at Mateo like he can take over, and then walks back to his classroom.

I escape into the bathroom and lock myself in a stall so I can smoke. No one gives a fuck if I smoke in here. There are no teachers patrolling hallways. If that science teacher's expectations are low, the office staff's expectations are nonexistent.

This might be the most shocking thing about school here in Anaheim.

No one gives a fuck.

No one gives a fuck about the kids, no one gives a fuck about the curriculum, no one gives a fuck about the rules. Oh, unless the rules are seniors with seven extra credits have to take an entire year of math and science over again for no reason. Suddenly everyone gives a fuck about *that* rule.

Back in Ohio everyone gave a fuck.

I'm not judging too harshly, either. I'm not overreacting. I've been to three high schools in California since I got here a year ago, and each one has some non-fuck-giving staff trying to make *me* give a fuck.

Why should I give a fuck?

I think I'll just continue to say fuck in my thoughts all day long. Maybe that will make me give a fuck?

"You're stupid, Shannon," I whisper to myself as I smoke. But it makes me smile. I check my phone and I'm already late for trig. It's five-twenty. Maybe Mateo went home?

God, I hope he went home. I don't know why I'm so pissed off, but I am. I'm pissed about everything. The credits thing, the night school shit, the teacher calling me on my temper tantrum, Mateo and his weirdness.

And Danny.

I'm pissed about Danny, I realize. Because I like him. And that story Mary told about him coming to her rescue as a little kid, well, it clinched it for me. He's not as bad as he looks. I felt it immediately when I met his eyes in the counselors office on Monday. He was sympathetic to my plight.

He gave a fuck.

So why does Mateo's warning unsettle me so much?

There's a knock at the door but I say nothing, just lean against the yellow cinderblock wall, smoking my cigarette.

"Shannon?" Mateo asks from the door. "I can smell the cigarette in the hallway, I know you're in here."

"I need the night off."

"Why?"

"I'm not in the mood for your shit or your head games. I worked ahead anyway. I've gotten five chapters outlined already."

"Trying to get it all done so you don't have to come here anymore?"

"What do you think?"

"I don't think it will be as easy to breeze through trig like you did science."

I blow out smoke rings as my response. "You're a fucking genius."

"Why are you so pissed off?"

"Why?" I huff out some air. "Just go away, Mateo. I'm not coming to class today."

A second later the door closes with a soft whoosh.

Well, mission accomplished. I wait in there, smoking my brains out, until the whole building goes silent. And thank God, when I finally decide to leave, the hallways are empty.

This has been the longest week of my life and it's not even Friday. I push through the front doors and a weight lifts off me. Mateo is stressing me out. That's why I'm mad. Mateo and his rules. Mateo and his weirdness. Mateo and his fucking dick.

God.

I have a problem. A really big problem. And it's not Mateo. My problem is me.

Jason is drunk when I get home. "Nice," I sneer at him. Olivia is awake, but Jason has a bottle of formula propped up on a blanket and she's slurping quietly in her swing. "I guess you won't be needing my services for much longer. Not after you get fired for showing up drunk tonight."

He drags his glazed eyes from the TV and stares at me in the chair to his right. "Be careful, kid. If you start nagging me like a wife, I'll start expecting more than just babysitting."

"You try it, I'll cut your dick off when you're sleeping."

"Tough girl, huh?" he says back, taking another swig of beer.

"People underestimate me all the time, Jason. You have no idea who I am. So feel free to join the rest of the world. You'll see what happens if you ever lay another hand on me."

He gets up, throws his empty bottle in the trash with a clang that says it's not his first today, and then grabs his keys and walks to the door. "You're so dramatic, Shannon. It's not my fault you fuck every guy you meet on the first date."

"Oh, is that what you think?"

"Jill talked just as much shit about you as you do about her. I know exactly who you are." He walks out the door, slamming it behind him.

Olivia starts and begins to cry. "Shhhh," I say to her, taking the bottle and lifting her out of that damn swing. I hold her close, rocking her a little as she rests her head on my chest. Poor baby. She's stuck with him and she has no idea what kind of a piece of shit he really is. "I won't leave you here," I tell her softly. "I promise. I won't leave you here."

We sit on the couch and mindlessly watch TV together. Well, she drinks her bottle and I do the mindless stuff. And before long she's her usual sleepy self. I take her back to

Jason's room and place her in her crib, covering her with a light blanket.

When I get back to the living room my phone is chiming a message.

Mateo: Did you eat?

Shannon: No.

I've been using the money Jason leaves on the counter for me for bus fare and school lunch all week. I haven't eaten since last night. I'm secretly hoping for a dinner invite when Mateo messages back.

Mateo: Check the back porch.

I get up and walk to the sliding door and look down at the ground where a brown paper bag is sitting. I open the door and look to my right, trying to see if he's in the alley beyond the gate, but there's nothing there.

I grab the bag and go inside, my mouth watering before I even set it on the counter. There's another note stapled to the bag, so I rip it off and open it up.

Remind me to remind you to tell me about how people underestimate you all the time.

Jesus Christ. He's watching me. Listening, at the very least. I bet he came over with food and stood right outside the slider.

I sigh, take out the food—leftover lasagna, hot—and get a fork. I can't shovel that stuff in my face fast enough, that's how hungry I am. I'm lucky if I eat once a day. I've never been this skinny in my life. I've lost so much weight since we moved to California, I'm probably about a hundred pounds. Which doesn't look bad on me, since I'm so short. But my stomach hurts every day from hunger. I just smoke to forget about it. I always have those, Jason has cartons of them on top of the fridge and for whatever reason, he doesn't bitch about me taking them, so I help myself daily.

You'd think that asshole would at least bring food home from the restaurant, but no. He doesn't.

My phone rings and I fish it out of my pocket and press accept. "Yeah," I say.

"Hungry much?"

I turn around and look at the back patio. Mateo is leaning against the chain-link fence that separates him from a hundred cars a second whizzing past on the freeway below. He looks like he hasn't got a care in the world.

"You're a creep, you know that?"

"Yeah, probably."

"What do you want?"

"No thank you?"

"Thanks," I mumble, then let out a long sigh. "Really, I mean it. Thanks. I was starving."

"I can tell. So you wanna tell me what that little meltdown was in school today?"

I just stare at him through the glass. "Why are you here? Why are you doing all this shit?"

"Are you going to finish that science work soon?"

"What?" *Nice,* I think. *Change the subject as soon as it comes back to you.*

"Shannon," he starts. "Don't ask me *what* when you hear me just fine."

"Yes," I snap. "I'm going to finish that fucking science."

"Good," he says. "We'll have class tomorrow at Gilbert. I've got a story to tell you. Make sure you're there."

And then he ends the call and walks off.

I enter Gilbert School at three-oh-five and make my way back to the class. There's a few people in the office today, and one classroom towards the front with kids in there working quietly. When I get to room twenty-one, Mateo is sitting at the desk reading a book.

I rest my backpack against the leg of the desk and sit in the chair opposite him.

"You going to finally teach me something today? I've outlined seven chapters in that book already."

He peers at me over the top of his book, which has the title *Exoplanets and Alien Solar Systems* on the cover.

"I've taught you a lot already. But I can understand why you're missing the point."

"Right. Don't flatter yourself, Mateo. I knew how to fuck before you showed up."

He puts his book down. "I have no doubt."

My face goes red. I wonder if he heard Jason basically call me a slut last night.

"Do you know what an exoplanet is?"

"No," I sneer.

"Hmm," he says, "too bad. It's pretty interesting."

"You said you had a story," I remind him. "Something about why you have take-out containers and food delivery bags." I've already worked out that his parents probably owned an Italian restaurant and that's why he can cook lasagna from scratch and has takeaway bags.

"Oh, that's not the story," he says, putting the book down. His hand goes to his belt and he starts unfastening it. It jingles a little and I just stare at him with an incredulous look.

"What the fuck are you doing?" I look over my shoulder at the open door. "I'm not fucking you here again. You can forget it. I'm not fucking you ever again, in fact. I'm done playing this sick game. I'm probably gonna date Danny Alexander," I say, lifting my chin up in defiance. "He's nice and he makes me laugh."

"Is that all it takes, Shannon? To win you over? A laugh?" He pops the button on his jeans and drags his zipper down so slowly, I can almost hear each interlocking piece disengage. I watch the movement of his arm as he pulls out his cock and fists it, pumping up and down slowly.

"About a month ago I saw you walking to Bill's. I followed you there, watched you eat a burger. Jose was nice to you, and that got me thinking. I know Jose. I know Jason, and Phil, and Mark at the arcade across from Anaheim. We all went to school together."

He's still masturbating as he talks, but sorta halfheartedly.

"So I asked him about you after you left. Told me you were Jason's sister-in-law, that he was back in town and living in those apartments across the way from my house."

"You're been spying on me. Got it."

"You walked over there a lot," he says, ignoring my comment. "So I had a lot of chances to follow you. I worked out where you lived, which window was yours on that patio facing the alley. And one night, I looked in and you were sleeping."

"Creep," I mutter. "You're such a creep."

"You guys never lock your patio door, did you know that?"

I get a sick feeling in my stomach.

"So one night I walked right in. Right into your bedroom. You were wearing a black tank top and just your underwear. Pink, they were," he says, smiling at me.

My mouth is open in shock. "You were in my bedroom?"

"And holy fuck, Shannon, you were so goddamned hot. And you'd been drinking, I think. You were sleeping pretty good."

I rack my brain, trying to figure out if I ever went home drunk in the last month. Maybe once, twice at the most. I haven't been partying a lot since I don't have many friends.

"So I started touching you."

"What?"

He's pumping his cock harder now and his breath is coming faster. He drags his white t-shirt up his stomach, exposing his abs to me.

"First, it was just a soft fingertip tracing the curve of your thigh. It made you shiver. And then you opened your legs and I did the same thing on the inside of your thigh."

I catch a glimpse of his swollen head each time his fist slides down his shaft. His eyes are closed now. There's voices in the hallway, and I have a brief moment of panic that we will get caught. That I will be blamed for letting him jerk off in front of me at school.

"I took my sweep a little higher each time, until finally I was fingering you through your pink panties. They were wet, Shannon. You were wet for me in your sleep."

The voices in the hallway recede, but I am speechless at this point. I would not be able to talk, even if I wanted to interrupt him. And I don't. Want to interrupt him, I mean. I want to hear every word.

"Very carefully I pulled your panties aside and began to play with you. You moaned in your sleep. Groaned, even. Like you wanted more. And you were so fucking wet, my fingers slipped right inside."

I think I'm at that same level of wetness right now.

He stops talking, pumping his cock harder now. I strain to get a better look at what he's doing. His legs are open, spread out under the table. Our legs are touching, in fact.

"And then I leaned down, pressed my lips to your pussy, and ate you out."

He groans and pumps himself furiously for a few seconds before spilling his come all over his bare stomach.

"You came," he says, after a few moments of rest. His eyes open and he looks straight at me. "You came in my mouth."

I just stare back. Unable to talk. Unable to comprehend what he's saying. "You're a liar."

He smiles. "But I'm a good one, right?"

"What?"

"You believed me. And you know why you believed me, Shannon?"

"That never happened?"

He scoffs. "Please, how drunk would you have to be for me to suck you off and never wake you up? Do you know *why* you believed me?"

"You're a psycho," I say, floored.

"Because you *want* to believe me."

I shake my head slowly. "I don't believe you. You're a very good liar, Mateo. And that's not something to be proud of."

"Right. So why are you so sure Danny Alexander is the nice one, and not me?"

"Because look at you," I scoff. "You're such a fucking freak."

"I'm sitting here in a chair, masturbating as I tell you a fantasy, Shannon. It's hot." And then he laughs. "You know it is."

"It's weird," I say. "I'm speechless with you most of the time because you're blowing my fucking mind. You make no sense to me. You don't follow the rules."

"Whose rules? Your rules?"

"School rules, for one. You're my fucking teacher!"

"Technically, no. I'm a subcontractor. But ethically, yes."

"It's the ethics that count, don't you think?"

"So walk out. Report me to Bowman. Call the police. Do whatever the fuck you want."

My thoughts are racing around in my head. "Maybe I will."

"At least you'd be invested. At least you'd stop just sitting here, begging me to get you out of this."

"Beg you!" Holy shit. "To get me out of what?" I just want to punch him in the fucking face right now.

"Life."

"OK," I huff. "I'm done here." I push my chair back to stand, but his words stop me.

"You want to skate through school, you said, take tests and call it learning. You want the prize without the work that goes into it. You want things you don't deserve."

"You don't know what I deserve," I say quietly. "You have no idea what I deserve."

"I know," he says, nodding. "But I do know what you don't deserve. And you can deny it all you want, it won't change the fact that you didn't earn it. I'm asking you to earn it."

"Earn what, Mateo? You make no sense."

"It." he replies. And then he lifts his hands up towards the ceiling.

"What's any of this," I say, lifting my hands up in the same way, "have to do with sex?"

He just smiles. "Nothing at all. It's got nothing at all to do with sex. I just like you and I want to fuck you, and tease you, and play you. Not like that," he says, seeing the anger inside me building. "Not like a victim, Shannon. Like an instrument."

He reaches over for a roll of paper towels sitting on the table next to him, rips one off, and cleans up the mess on his stomach. He throws it into the trash, stands up, and puts himself back together.

"If you want to walk away," he says, grabbing his book from the table, "go ahead. Report me to Bowman, tell the police, do whatever the fuck you want. But I'm trying to tell you, I'm invested. So go date Danny Alexander if you want. You can quit this class and drop out of school. You can fuck everything up. You're a grown woman, you can make whatever choice you feel is best. But when you look back in ten years and wonder where it all went wrong, don't blame me, Shannon. Because I gave a fuck and you walked out."

And then *he* walks out. He's got that stupid book in his hand and he just walks out and leaves me there.

Stunned.

I sit in silence for, fuck—minutes, I think.

"You done in here?"

I whirl around in my chair and find the janitor peeking his head into the room.

"I'm locking up, kid. Time to go home."

I nod, dragging myself out of my stupor, and grab my backpack. I don't say a word as I walk past him and out of the school. It's dark already and the parking lot is empty. But off to the left I can hear the low rumble of a motorcycle.

I look over and see Mateo, helmet and leather jacket on, staring at me.

I walk towards him and stop a few feet away. He's holding out a flannel and a helmet. I take the flannel and slip it on, hiking my pack up onto my back, and then shove the helmet down on my head as I swing my leg over the seat.

I sigh as I press my cheek against his jacket, taking in the scent of him, and wrap my arms around his waist. He places a hand on mine for a second, and then we move forward and leave the school behind.

He doesn't take me home. He pulls into his driveway and I sit on the back of the bike as we wait for the garage to open. He pulls in, turns the bike off, and kicks down the stand.

There are at least half a dozen cars in his giant garage. All classics. An old Mustang, a classic Camaro, a GTO, and some more I can't easily identify, plus parts. The place is spilling over with cars and it's a lot bigger on the inside than it looks on the outside. I get a sense that there is a lot more to Mateo Alesci than meets the eye. I don't know him any more than he knows me.

I take my helmet off and swing my leg over the bike. He does the same.

And we look at each other.

"You wanna go to the beach with me tomorrow night?" he asks.

I nod and place the helmet on his seat.

"Pick you up in front of your house at seven."

He walks away and goes inside his house.

I'm barely aware of the traffic on Broadway as I cross the street, walk through the gate of the apartments that are not mine, enter the alley on the other side, and make my way to my patio. I have to lean against the brick wall next to my window and take a few deep breaths.

I don't know anything right now. I'm blown. I go inside and I don't even hear Jason's snide remarks as he gathers his keys and walks out, leaving me with a sleeping Olivia.

I am blown.

20

I have been babysitting on Saturdays ever since Jill died. Jason always works breakfast and lunch on the weekends and he leaves early in the morning. But Olivia woke up around three AM and didn't stop crying. When I went into Jason's room to see what the problem was, he wasn't there. He never came home. Asshole. I'm so fucking pissed about that. Responsible people don't stay out all night when they have a baby at home.

And she's been cranky all day too. I'm just starting to wonder if I should take her temperature and see if she's sick or something when at ten minutes to seven, Jason walks in looking like total shit.

"Where the fuck have you been?"

"Working," he sneers, walking into the kitchen. "Foreign concept, I know." He starts making Olivia a bottle.

"She already has a bottle, Jason. She might be sick."

"You just make it wrong."

"OK," I say, grabbing my purse. "I'm out of here." I go out the back way, like normal—I don't like the thought of Jason watching me out the front window as I wait for Mateo. It creeps me out far more than anything that's happened between me and my teacher. I walk back up the alley to the laundry building and slip through the passageway that leads back to the front.

"Hey, Shannon," a woman says off to my left.

Shit, that cop chick. I nod and keep walking.

"How's your niece?""

"What?" I ask, stopping to turn.

"The baby. I heard her crying today. Is everything OK?"

"Oh, yeah," I say, letting out a sigh. "She was fussy all day. But Jason's home now, he'll get her to sleep. He's good at it." He is too. I have to reluctantly admit that.

"Good to hear," she says. "See you around. Don't get in any trouble tonight."

"Right," I say, just as Mateo's car pulls up on the far side of the quad. It's the red Camaro I saw in the garage and it's rumbling like a monster. He gets out and walks around to the passenger side, opening my door for me. I take him in, I can't help it. He's wearing a black t-shirt, leather jacket, jeans and boots. Same old, same old. But for some reason, he looks different.

"Subtle," I say, motioning to the loud-as-fuck car and slipping into the seat. I catch a smile as he closes the door and watch him under the streetlights as he walks around to his side and gets back in.

"Did you eat?" he asks.

"No."

"Doesn't that fuck feed you?"

I scoff. "Why would he?" And then I sigh again. Jesus, I'm in a bad mood. "He does give me money sometimes. But the only food he buys is formula for Olivia. I guess he eats at the restaurant."

"What restaurant?" Mateo asks, pulling away from the curb and flipping a bitch to head back towards West Street.

"Oh, I don't even know. I guess he works somewhere over by Disneyland. He's a chef."

"He's a chef?" Mateo says with disbelief.

"Yeah, why?"

"Nothing. Just interesting."

"Where are we going?" I ask, a few blocks later when he gets on the freeway.

"Crescent Bay in Laguna."

"Why so far? We could just go to the fire pits at Huntington."

"You can't see the stars in Huntington. Even with a new moon."

"You're taking me to see the stars?" I have to look away to hide my smile.

"So you wanna eat before or after?"

"Dinner too?"

He laughs. "God, Shannon. You act like you've never been on a date before."

"This is a date?"

"Isn't it?" he asks, squinting at me. "I guess I wasn't clear."

I stay silent for a few seconds, mulling this over. I hadn't really thought about it as a date. "Well, wow."

"Wow what?"

"I just didn't expect it, that's all."

"You thought I was a fuck-'em-and-forget-'em kind of guy? You don't listen very well, do you?"

"I hear you, Mateo. I just don't *believe* you."

"Fair enough. Everyone's got baggage. But you have to believe in someone eventually. It might as well be me."

"You lied last night. You had me freaking out that you were in my bedroom touching me while I was sleeping."

"It turned you on. You can admit it, you know."

"It freaked me out, Mateo."

"Sure did," he says. "It freaked you out so much you got on my bike ten minutes later. It freaked you out so much you agreed to go on a date with me. So why did you do those things if you think I'm creepy?"

I can't answer that.

"Do you really need me to state the obvious?"

"Yes," I say back. "I really do."

"You like me."

"I think I'm afraid of you, Mateo."

"Then why are you here?" he asks. It's not a confrontational question, either. It comes off as sincere. Like he needs to know the answer as much as I do. "Why not just go out with Danny Alexander?"

I sigh heavily.

"I'm gonna make you admit it tonight, so go ahead, get it over with."

"Maybe I just want to graduate high school and I need you to help me do that."

"I'm pretty sure Bowman would find you another teacher if you told him what was going on."

Another heavy sigh from me.

"Just say it," he says softly. "I'm dying to hear the words, Shannon. And once you say them out loud, you'll feel better."

But I don't say them. I know he wants me to admit that I like this. But I'm just not sure I do. He's confusing me. He mixing up the school work with the sex, even though the other day he said they are not related. He's making them related. He's tying my need to finish this class in with his desire to control me.

So I keep quiet and he turns some music on—Cage the Elephant, by some stupid twist of fate—and I just stare out at the other cars on the freeway. It takes a good half hour to get to Laguna and the town is bustling with people out for the evening. We park the car and get out, Mateo grabbing a backpack stuffed with things and slinging it over his shoulder as he takes my hand.

Takes. My. Hand.

I look down at it.

"You don't like the hand-holding?" he asks, as we walk through the small grassy area towards the steps that will take us down to the beach.

"I just *don't understand* the hand-holding."

"It's a pretty basic display of affection, Shannon. Not real complicated."

"Ummm. It's very complicated when you're fucking your teacher who is ten years older than you."

He lets go of my hand. "OK."

I sigh. Jesus Christ. Why did I even come out with him tonight? Why the hell am I even talking to this creep? He's probably a serial killer. He probably likes weird sex with butt plugs and whips.

"Do you know what the new moon is?"

I roll my eyes. "I might only be eighteen but I'm not an idiot."

"I have never thought you were an idiot, Shannon Drake. Ever. So do you know what it is?" he repeats.

"There's no moon on the new moon."

"But you probably don't know why, right? Most people don't understand the movement of the moon, and that's cool, because it's sorta complicated. That's all I'm asking, Shannon. Why do you get so defensive?"

"Why do you make me feel so stupid?"

"Do I?" he asks. "It's not one of my goals with you, so take that any way you want."

I say nothing after that. I'm too busy noticing how fucking dark and empty of people it is down here on the beach. It's winter, for one. And cold in a SoCal kind of way. Regardless of what people think, the beach isn't somewhere people go on winter nights.

We walk out to the middle of the beach and he unpacks a blanket and throws it down on the sand. "Come on," he says, lowering himself down. I just stand there as he takes his shoes off.

"Are you going to fuck me out here?"

He laughs. "I wasn't planning on it, but hey, I won't turn you down if you insist."

I lower myself to my knees and sit back on my butt.

"Take off your shoes, for fuck's sake. It's the beach."

I reposition myself and take off my Chucks, and then stretch out my legs next to his as he lies back and puts his hands behind his neck. I follow along, doing the same.

"So that orange star right there," he says, pointing up at the sky, "is Aldebaran. It's in the constellation Taurus."

"Hmmm," I say, trying to find which of the many points of light he's talking about. "I can't tell which one is which."

"Look at that row of stars right there." He points. "Those three that are bright and close together, that's Orion's Belt."

"OK, I see those."

"Go up and to the right, that bright orange one is Aldebaran."

"Got it."

"And if you drop down to the left again, right below Orion's Belt, that's Rigel. And if you go over to the left even more, that bright blue one is Sirius. Have you heard of any of these?" he asks.

"Sirius. And Orion's Belt, of course. But I've never looked up and seen them in person before."

"Aldebaran is sixty-five point two three light years away from Earth. Sirius is eight point six eleven. Sirius is the brightest star in the sky because it's one of the closest stars to Earth. It would be easy to conclude that Sirius is *the* closest star to Earth, since it's the brightest. But you can't rely on brightness to prove distance, because not all stars are the same size, and of course, size does matter."

I chuckle with him over the sex joke.

"The purpose of trig is to find distances by using the sides of a triangle, which are based on circles. So in astronomy we use a certain form of it to find distances between stars, or how far away a star is from the Sun or some other celestial object."

"Are you really talking about math right now?"

"Why not? You seem to be fixated on my role as your teacher. I'm a good teacher, Shannon. You should give me a chance."

"I totally give up, Mateo. You officially win. Because I just don't understand you." I look over at him and he's smiling so big I have to shake my head and laugh. "What?"

"I wore you down?"

"Just—fuck. You're not like anyone I've ever met before. You are seriously the strangest person ever."

"Anyway," he says with a chuckle. "Trig is about circles and triangles. And they are related by drawing lines that originate from the center."

"Blah, blah, blah," I say. "I don't want to hear this."

"Why not?"

"Because that's all I hear when you say things like circle and triangles. Blah, blah, blah. I know you people think I'm smart for some reason—"

"Which is funny, since you just accused me of making you feel dumb."

"—but I officially cheated my way through those classes."

"I get that. But I'm not letting you cheat your way through this one. So shut up and listen. Because you say you want me to teach you how to work the problems out so you get the right answer, but you don't want to understand the answer or how you got it. Right?"

"Right. It's just easier."

"Well, of course it's fucking easier, but it's meaningless, Shannon. Don't you get it yet?"

"No." I laugh. "I don't."

"I know," he says, turning towards me, leaning on his elbow and propping his head up with his hand. "I'm confusing you, right? You don't understand my intentions. You don't know what I'm doing. Why are we having sex?"

"I don't know." I laugh again. "I really don't."

"That's because you're trying to get the answer without trying to understand the process of how to find it."

I just look at him. "Are you fucking kidding me right now? Are you seriously trying to say you're confusing me with sex to teach me a lesson in math?"

"Your question," he says, ignoring that statement, "is something along the lines of, what am I doing? But that's the wrong question. Your real question is, why am I doing it?"

"You've been fucking with me on purpose."

"And the answer you're so desperate to find is, because Mateo likes me. You want that to be the answer so bad, you stick around, letting me do all these things, with the hope that I'll eventually say it."

"You did say it. A few times, at least."

"But you didn't believe me."

"Why should I? You were lying."

"How do you know I was lying?"

"You told me you made that story up yesterday."

"So maybe the question is, why did I make that story up?"

"To come in front of me? Put me off my guard? Get off? I don't know."

"Do you really think I just go around making up fantasies with every girl I meet so I can come in front of them?"

He stares at me. Those green eyes looking into me. Searching inside of me. Seeing through me like I'm a gaping hole.

"Why are you doing it, Mateo?"

"Tell me why I'm doing it, Shannon."

I could fight it out with him. Point out all the ways that he's being an asshole. How he's confusing me and making things difficult. But there's only one real answer to that question, and it's very simple. "You like me."

"And?" he prods. "That's not all. I can show you I like you a million different ways. I could just rescue you from the rain or feed you lasagna if all I wanted to do was show you I like you."

I give up. He really does win. Maybe he's an evil genius and he pulled this plan out of his ass after the fact. He is some kind of physicist, right? He's probably capable. But he was there the morning I lost my shit with Bowman and confessed that I was half-assing my way through school. He started the inappropriate touching the first time we met by stretching his legs out under the table. He fucked me in the classroom the very next day. He had me off my half-assing game from the moment he plunked that folder down on Bowman's desk to this very second. And he did it all with an end in mind.

"I can't understand the answer to my problem unless I understand the process of working it out. Are you my problem, Mateo? Or my answer?"

"Which do you want me to be?"

"Both."

"Fuck," he yells, lying back on the blanket and holding his hands out towards the sky like he's giving thanks. "Holy fuck." And then he laughs. "Finally."

"You are the biggest asshole ever."

"Thank you," he says, still laughing.

"I think I hate you right now."

"I don't care," he says, turning over on his stomach and resting his head in his hands so he can see my face. "You'll love me in the end."

21

"Do you want to hear the real story of how I first saw you?"

We've been lying here in silence for a few minutes. I've been looking up at the stars and he's been looking at me. I guess he figured I needed a little time to wrap my head around his methods. "Yes," I say, still lost in thought.

"I was sitting on my porch, rebuilding the carburetor for the Camaro. This was last month."

I turn over on my stomach and rest my cheek on my hands so I can watch him as he talks.

"And I saw this girl come out of the gate from the apartments across Broadway. She was wearing a black leather jacket that screamed *chick* and *don't fuck with me* at the same time. I haven't seen you wear it again, but I dig the belt."

"It's too hot here," I say. "I'm used to the cold."

"And she had on some ripped jeans and black Chucks," he says, picking up one of my shoes and waving it for a second. "Her long brown hair was fanning out behind her, blowing in the wind. And she was walking across the bridge over the 5 like she was the boss of the world."

I chuckle at that image.

"Like she was daring it to come mess with her, she had a lesson to teach it. You told me you felt invisible when that girl spoke to you in Spanish, right? Like she talked to you before, but she never saw you. And that day it was all too much. She missed it. She missed everything that made you you. But she didn't talk to you in Spanish because she *missed* you, Shannon. You're an unmissable girl. You're a fucking explosion in a bottle waiting to happen. People talk to you because they can't help but *see* you."

"You're stupid."

"Anyway, back to my story about that girl. I swear to God, I got up off my porch and I followed her. She didn't go far, just over the bridge to the burger place. And I know Jose, so I went over and by the time I got there, she was sitting at a table in the back, waiting for her food. I ordered a burger too, and sat near the front, facing her, so I could get a better look. And I noticed that she dropped her bossy attitude with Jose when he came with her meal. She liked him, I could tell. He's married, has a pot belly and was covered in grease, so I figured that she considered him a friend and was not interested in fucking him on the table."

"Jesus, Mateo. Please. I don't need that visual."

"And I thought to myself, *I need to be her friend.* I never missed you, Shannon. I saw you immediately and I wanted to be your friend."

I smile at that. So much better than *I need to fuck her in a classroom.*

"She ate, walked home. I followed behind, watched her go back into the apartment. So I went through the gate and saw her exit on the other side of the pool where the alley was. And when I got to the alley, she was gone. Just poof, disappeared."

"I was already on my patio."

"Right. And then I got this call from Bowman the next day asking me did I want a job teaching trig to a student who needed to make up a credit in order to graduate. He told me the whole credit situation and I was like, shit, I dunno. I have this dissertation to write. I don't think I have time. But he said just stop by school on January fourth and I could meet you. He told me you needed help. Like, really needed help. He told me about your sister and Jason. The kid, all of it."

"What a dick. I hate people talking about me."

"So I dropped by and I came in just as you sat down to talk. And I swear to God, I lost my breath when I realized you were her. So I took the job and I promised Bowman I'd help you." He smiles at me and I might just fall in love. "But I heard you begging to get out of the class and I decided to make you mine and make you learn at the same time."

"It's pretty unorthodox. We could get caught."

"Do we care, Shannon? Do we care if we get caught?"

"I don't think so," I answer, chuckling.

"I don't give a fuck if we get caught, obviously. But I do give a fuck if you don't graduate. So I hope we don't until you finish the work. I'd never forgive myself if I fucked up your graduation."

"Then why risk it?"

"Because I saw Danny Alexander sitting next to you in the office. And he was looking at you the same way I was. And there was no way I'd let him have you. No fucking way."

"I saw you that day too."

153

"Yeah?" He smiles. And if I'm not mistaken, he looks like he really needs to know what I thought of him. My stomach flutters and I start to see things differently.

"You had that leather jacket on and those fuck-hot biker boots. I think I stopped breathing for a second."

"And then you saw me in the classroom and wanted to fall to your knees and kiss the ground, thanking God for your good fortune?"

"Yeah." I laugh. "That's exactly how it happened."

"And when I pushed my leg against yours, you pulled away. And when I did it again, you let me."

"I didn't know what to do!"

"And you went on and on about how you weren't smart and I thought to myself, *That's fucked up.* Because obviously no one in your past wanted to take the time to set you straight. So I made it my mission to teach you a lesson."

"I'm smart."

"You're smart. You passed geometry by taking a bet. You aced a final exam, for fuck's sake. Don't sell yourself short, Shannon. You can do trig. Hell, you can do calculus too, if you set your mind to it."

"Well, I'm not sure I agree with your methods, Mr. Alesci, but I do agree with your assessment."

He laughs and leans over to kiss me. I get lost in that moment. I get stranded there on the beach with him like we're alone on a deserted island, drifting in a sea of stars.

He slips an arm under me, bringing me closer, our mouths never parting as we fill the need inside us. The kiss is slow and soft. It's not about the taboo romance we're having. It's not about the shock value. It's not about lessons learned or the future.

It's just about right now.

We stop kissing and take a moment to see each other. Like really see each other. "Are you hungry?" he asks.

"Starving," I say. "But not just for food."

"Let's go eat."

We rise and I help him fold the blanket back up. And this time when he takes hold of my hand, I let him.

We walk back to the car, put his backpack in the trunk, and he points to the shops at the end of the street. "I know a place."

I bet he does. He seems to know everything.

He pulls out and we make our way onto Pacific Coast Highway going south, and a few miles later he pulls into a restaurant valet and two men approach our car and pull open our doors.

"Good evening, Mr. Alesci," the one on his side says.

"Ma'am," the one on my side says.

I barely manage a, "Thank you," as I exit the car and wait at the curb, while Mateo talks into the other valet's ear and hands him some cash. He pats him on the back and walks over to me, taking my hand.

"Ready?" he asks, weaving us through a crowd of people waiting to get inside.

"What's going on here?"

"Just don't look up."

Of course I look up. And see the name of the restaurant above the door. "Alesci's Laguna Beach?"

"Whatever you do, don't show fear."

"Mateo—"

But an older woman interrupts me. She places her hands on his cheeks and spills out something in Italian. He

155

blushes. I laugh. And then he's talking in Italian a mile a minute as the woman takes me in and gives me a very suspicious look.

"Mom—"

Jesus Christ. You have got to be kidding me. Mateo's mother is tall and thin, wearing a designer suit and diamonds everywhere I look. Her hair is a rich mahogany brown, her makeup is perfect, her shoes probably cost more than, well, everything I own, plus a few thousand dollars more, and she smells like a very expensive bottle of perfume.

"—this is Shannon."

"Shannon?" she says, like she's never heard the name before in her life. I'm not Italian and no amount of wishing will change that.

"We're just here to eat dinner. I called ahead and Vinnie set us a table upstairs."

I might get a mother's evil eye from that statement. "Um," I say, way, way out of my comfort zone. "Nice to meet you, Mrs. Alesci."

She gives me another once-over but Mateo has me by the hand and he's practically dragging me to the back of the restaurant. We climb the stairs, which are narrow, so there is nothing to do but keep hold of his hand as he leads me, and then find ourselves out on a private patio where there are about half a dozen empty tables and only one is set for dinner.

Mateo pulls my chair out and I sit, watching him as he takes the seat across from me.

"What the hell did you just do?" I ask.

"What?" he says innocently.

"Tell me that didn't just happen."

"You met my mother, so what?"

"I'm ten fucking years younger than you, Mateo," I whisper-yell. I might be having a panic attack. "This is not cool."

"Why not?" The waiter comes up the stairs and Mateo holds up two fingers. "Vino and lasagna bolognese." The waiter nods and goes back down.

"Oh, my God, did you just order me wine? Your mother is going to kill me."

"Don't be ridiculous," he says, leaning over the table to kiss me on the cheek. "She loves me too much to kill you, Shannon."

I just shake my head at him. "I cannot believe you brought me here."

"Why?"

"Mateo, you're twenty-eight. I'm eighteen."

"Eighteen is the key number. She'll be fine. Just relax. Besides, what kind of date would it be if I didn't keep you on your toes?"

I'm just about to answer when an older man comes up and squeezes Mateo's shoulder, babbling in Italian.

I just smile and nod. This is a nightmare.

"Be right back," Mateo says, getting up. "I have to go say hi to my aunt." His fingertips brush my shoulder as he walks past me and then he disappears down the stairs.

"Great," I mutter, wringing my hands in my lap.

"Shannon."

I turn around and yup, right on cue, there's the mom coming to check me out. I have a moment of rage that Mateo fell for it, and then roll my eyes, because yeah, like that was what happened. He left me up here on purpose so she could come grill me.

"Um, hi!" I try to say it brightly. "Mrs. Alesci. You have a very nice restaurant."

"May I?" she asks, waving her hand at Mateo's chair.

"Well…" I laugh nervously. "I suppose that's why Mateo left so suddenly, so of course."

She smiles sweetly at me, folding her hands on the table. "Just one question."

"Eighteen," I blurt.

She laughs, gets back up and walks away. I watch her retreat down the stairs, but just as quickly she turns and starts walking back up.

Shit. I take a deep breath and stand, read to bolt downstairs if she starts smacking me. I once dated an Italian guy back in Ohio and I can say from experience, these mamas do not fuck around when it comes to their sons.

But she walks towards me smiling, holding her hands out and reaching for mine. She squeezes them both at the same time, then leans in to kiss me on both cheeks. "I'm Mateo's mother, Gigi Alesci, and you may call me Gigi. I'm so happy to meet you, Shannon."

Oh, my God, the weirdness runs in the family. "I know, I just met you down—"

"We needed a new start," she says, interrupting me. "I was a little shocked downstairs, but you can't hold it against me. You are very young."

"I totally understand," I say. "I had no idea he was bringing me here. Actually, I had no idea his family had a restaurant." Shit, I just lied to his mother. "Well, I had some idea."

"Relax," she says. "I'm not here to pry. I'm just as surprised as you, because my dear, he has never brought a girl to Alesci's Laguna Beach. This," she stresses, "this is the *serious* restaurant."

"Oh. I was hungry and we were in the neighborhood. He took me to the beach to look at the stars."

"No, my dear," she says, shaking her head. "I'm sure he's in the neighborhood a lot. That's not why he brought you here." She tilts her head and her smile widens. "We have seven Alesci's Restaurants in Southern California and only one where I work every night. He brought you to meet me."

"I have nothing for that," I lie again, and then blurt. "I just met him. He's my teacher, and I'm sorry—he's weird, but I like him."

She laughs so hard she has to cover her mouth.

"What? Oh, my God, what did I do?"

"I like you, Shannon. Please," she says, rising as I spot Mateo coming towards us. "Enjoy the food."

They speak again in Italian, part with a kiss to each cheek, and then Mateo walks back over to me and sits down and places a bottle of wine on the table. "Drink?" he asks.

I nod dumbly. "I think I might need one." He laughs. It's that laugh I like. "Who are you? And what did you do with Mateo?"

"She was nice, right?"

"She just wanted to know how old I was."

"I figured."

"But yes, she was nice. She said you brought me here to meet her."

"I did," he says, pouring the wine. "And if you think it's over, just prepare yourself."

"What?"

But as soon as the word leaves my mouth, three younger women come up the stairs, laughing and giggling.

"Shannon, allow me to introduce my cousins, Gina, Beth, and Lori."

I lose track of the family members after that. There is no hope for me at all. They come up to the terrace in packs, and clearly this is either a family-only dining area or the only people who eat at Alesci's Laguna Beach are related, because everyone up there is introduced with a title. Brother-in-law, aunt, cousin, niece, nephew, granddad, and uncle.

We don't get one second alone. And they grill me, but in the nicest way.

"What do you do?"

"She graduates high school this semester."

I get a few looks from that, but they move on. "What will you study after high school? Will you move away? Do you want children?"

Mateo fields that one with something in Italian, and I have to take a deep breath to try to stop the building panic. The food arrives and we eat as they continue talking.

And hours later, I'm partially drunk, I've eaten so much I want to take my pants off at the table, and my eyes begin to droop.

"Well," Mateo says, standing up and walking around to get my chair, "we've got to get home." There's a rush of people who kiss me on both cheeks and tell me to come back soon.

I leave there with a longing in my heart and a hole in my soul.

Is this what it's like to have a family?

I don't have much to compare it to, but I decide it is, and I decide I like it, and I decide I want it.

I want him.

When we get home, and I get out of the car, I wish so bad that he'd invite me in and keep me forever. The last thing I want to do is go home to Jason.

But he doesn't. He takes my hand and walks me across the street. He pushes me against the brick wall just a few inches from my bedroom window and kisses me goodnight.

I go inside feeling sadder than I have a right to.

22

Mateo didn't call on Sunday, and if that was all that happened in the days following our 'date', I'd get over it. But he never showed for class on Monday. I took the bus all the way over to Gilbert only to find the doors locked. I waited, nothing. I took the bus home and texted him. Nothing.

The next day I had to show up for science class, so I took the bus out to Gilbert again, did my two hours, turned in several more open-book tests, and went to room twenty-one.

Empty and dark.

I texted again. Nothing.

So I got desperate and tried to call, but it went straight to voicemail.

What the fuck?

"Shannon?" A push on my shoulder takes my attention away from my phone and I look to see Sunday peering down at me. "Didn't you hear me? I called your name three times."

"Oh," I say, pointing to my ear. "I have an ear infection. It's all clogged up." I do too. It started on Sunday afternoon and it's been building ever since. "I get them a lot and the drops I had left over from the last one aren't working yet."

"Why do you look so unhappy?"

"I'm just in pain, that's all. I took some pills, but they're not working either."

"You looked this way yesterday too. There's something you're not telling me. What's going on?"

There's no one here but us. People ditched to go smoke out at the arcade across the street at lunch. I have some vague recollection of being asked to partake, but waving them off as I concentrated on Mateo's absence.

Obviously, I can't tell Sunday anything about Mateo. "I think I'm going home. It'll feel better tomorrow."

"I'll take you," he says.

I know I should say no, but the ear really does hurt. And the thought of walking the few blocks home makes me tired just standing here. "OK."

He takes my backpack and we walk towards the parking lot. "The ex-boyfriend giving you trouble?"

I sigh. "I don't want to talk about it."

"OK," he says again, opening the passenger door for me and placing my pack at my feet. He closes my door and walks around to get in his side, starts up the car and pulls out.

"It's just, we had a really good weekend. Saturday night was fun. And then Sunday, nothing. No call, no text. And I haven't been able to get a hold of him since. He's just disappeared."

"I thought you didn't want to talk about it?"

"Sorry," I say, placing a hand over my ear to try to dull the pain.

We drive in silence after that, and thankfully, a few minutes later, he pulls up in front of my apartments. "You gonna be OK?"

I nod as I gather my backpack and get out of the car. "Thank you. See you tomorrow."

He waits there at the curb until I get my key in the door, and then I wave for him to leave. Say what you will about Danny Alexander, but he's considerate.

A lot more considerate than Mateo right now.

Jason's not home, of course. And Olivia is at the sitter's. So it's nice to be here and not have to think of anyone but me. I head to my bed and crash out, hoping like hell this ear will get better instead of worse.

"Shannon."

The pain in my ear is unbearable.

"Shannon, goddammit!"

"Don't fucking yell at me, I'm sick." I open my eyes and Jason is standing over my bed, glaring down at me.

"Wake the fuck up, I have to go to work." He's swaying back and forth, that's how drunk he is.

"I can't watch her tonight, Jason. I'm in so much pain. I need to go to the doctor and get ear drops. My ear—"

"I'm not paying for a fucking doctor's visit for *you*. You're not my responsibility. You are living in my house, and you will be watching Olivia tonight because I have to go to work. So get the fuck up and take care of her."

He walks out. Not just out of my room, but out of the house, because he slams the door. It scares Olivia and she starts crying.

I get up.

Poor Olivia. I'm glad she's too little to understand what a messed-up life she's got right now. I pick her up and take her into the kitchen. She has little milk stains on her chin that I wipe with a warm washcloth, and then I take her to the couch, lie down, and pull her close to me.

We stay that way all night until Jason comes home at midnight and puts her to bed.

I gulp down a few more pills and go into my room. I find my phone on my pillow where I left it earlier in the day, and I have a moment of hope that Mateo called me back.

But I have no messages.

"Shannon?" But all I get is a muffled voice because my ear is so clogged up with shit. "Shannon," he repeats.

A hand rocks my shoulder and I open my eyes.

"Hey there, Daydreams," Sunday says. "Your slider door was unlocked so I came in to see if you were here. Sorry for breaking in, but you missed school today and I was worried."

I start crying. "My ear hurts, Danny. It hurts so bad and Jason won't take me to the doctor to get antibiotics."

"Shit," he says, sitting down on my futon next to me. "Let me see it." He gently moves my hair and I wince, that's how sensitive I am right now. "Aw, fuck. I think you need to go to the emergency room, Shannon. It's got green stuff bubbling out of it."

"I don't have any money," I sob. "And Jason won't pay for it."

"Don't worry about it, OK?" He squeezes my shoulder. "Come on, we're going now." He gets me up and helps me outside to his car in the alley and buckles me in the seat.

When he gets in on his side he frowns at me. "You should've called me. I'd have come and taken you."

"I should've," I say. "Thank you."

We drive over to the hospital in silence. He doesn't even turn the music on. And when we get to the ER, he helps me walk in and makes me sit down while he explains what's wrong.

We wait for almost an hour to be shown to a room, then another twenty minutes to be seen.

"Jesus Christ," the young doctor says, looking at my ear. "What happened?" He glares at Sunday like he's to blame for my condition.

"I get swimmer's ear at least twice a year. I just need some antibiotics and drops."

"Do you swim?"

They ask this every time. "No." And they always give me that same look. "I don't know why I get it, I just do. And I need drops and antibiotics to make it better. Can you please just write me a prescription?"

"We'll have to flush it out and—"

"No," I say. "That will hurt even more and make it worse. I've done this before. I'm telling you, I just need the drops and the antibiotics. I know how to fix it, I get these all the time."

"Look, kid, you can't get drops inside the ear canal unless I clean it out, so—"

"Hey," Sunday says, pushing the doctor away from me. "She said she needs drops and antibiotics. Just write the fucking prescriptions. The longer you stand here and argue about it, the longer she's in pain."

The doctor huffs. He looks young. I hate the young ones. They always have alternative ideas about why I get the infections and they always fuck it up even worse. "You're gonna have to wait outside."

"I'm not going anywhere," Sunday says, pushing the doctor in the chest. "She told you what the problem is, she told you she has a history of it, and if you don't write those prescriptions, I'm gonna go out in that hallway and find someone who will."

"They're not free, you know. And she has no insurance," the doctor says, glaring at Sunday. "We don't take indigent cases here. You're going to have to—"

Sunday takes out his wallet, opens it up, and shoves some bills into the doctor's chest. "She's not indigent, asshole. We're just paying cash. So write the fucking prescriptions and we'll leave you to your work."

They have one of those manly stand-offs, eyes blazing, egos rising, and chests practically bumping.

But Sunday stands his ground and the doctor pulls out his prescription pad. "I'm just trying to help you, kid. Your boyfriend isn't doing you any favors." He scribbles as he talks, ripping the prescriptions off one at a time. "I'll write you one for codeine too, to get you out of the pain."

"Thank you," I say. But I'm looking at Sunday when I say it.

Twenty minutes later I'm gulping pills outside the hospital pharmacy and Sunday is looking at me like I might die on him. "I'll be OK, I swear. You can take me home."

"I'm not dropping you at home. You're coming to stay with me until someone who gives more fucks than I do shows up to take over."

I don't argue. I just want to sleep this whole thing off and I do not care where I do that. I rest my head against the window, the daylight fading away with me as I drift off.

23

"Open the fucking door!"

I jolt upright in bed at the sound of Jason's voice. But then Danny is yelling back. There's a scuffle outside, like they're fighting. Someone gets knocked up against the door and it comes flying open.

Jason falls to the ground and looks at me. "What the fuck do you think you're doing?" he yells, getting to his feet and coming towards me. Danny grabs him by the shirt and throws him back to the ground.

"I told you to stay the fuck out of my house," Danny says. "Now you've got three seconds to get your ass out before I break one of your legs."

Jason gets back up, but his anger and glare are both directed at me. "You left me hanging, Shannon. You left me fucking hanging last night. As far as I'm concerned, you're done. Don't come home. And don't ever plan on seeing your niece again."

He pushes past Danny and we both stare at each other as Jason makes his way out of the house, slamming the door behind him.

"Fuck," Danny says. "Your brother-in-law is an asshole."

"I know," I say, letting out a long sigh.

"How you feeling?"

"Better," I say, touching my ear. "How long did I sleep?"

"About eighteen hours." Danny laughs. "It was probably the pills."

I look down at the bed, realize where I'm at, and then get up quickly, only to sit back down as my head spins.

"Hey," Danny says, coming over to steady me. "Just relax, man. Jason is full of shit. He's not kicking you out, he's not taking your niece away. He's just pissed off about his situation and he's taking it out on you. But believe me, when Phil finds out about this, he'll set him straight."

"What's Phil got to do with Jason?"

But before Danny can answer, Rocky is in the open doorway, knocking on the wall outside. "Sorry to interrupt, but Mateo Alesci is outside, Danny. And he's looking for Shannon."

Danny looks over at me, his eyes narrowing in understanding.

"OK," Rocky says. "I'm out of here. But you better go talk to him, Dan, because if Phil gets home and sees him in the driveway, there's gonna be blood."

Rocky leaves, pounding down the stairs. When she opens the door I can hear Mateo's voice, but then she closes it quickly and that fades.

"Please tell me Mateo Alesci is not the boyfriend."

I just stare at him.

"Jesus fucking Christ, Shannon. You're a goddamned mess. Do you even know who the fuck he is?"

I don't even know where to begin with that. "I'm sorry. I'll go." I stand up again, but Danny places both hands on my shoulders and pushes me back.

"Just stay here. I'll get rid of him. Unless you want to go down there, and then I'm out too and you're on your own tonight."

"No," I say. "I don't want to talk to anyone right now."

He nods. "OK. BRB." He pounds down the stairs too. The door down below opens and Mateo is immediately asking about me.

I get up and walk over to the window, looking out through the sheer white curtains. Mateo is mad, I can tell that much. But Danny stands his ground, shaking his head. They are about the same height, but Mateo has ten years on Danny and it shows in the bulk of his muscular body. Mateo's not wearing his leather jacket and jeans, like he normally does. Instead he's dressed in the remnants of a suit. White dress shirt, dark slacks, and a loose tie hanging around his neck.

Mateo glances up at the window, and I hold still, but he must not see me, because his attention goes back to Danny. He hands him something and then Mateo walks off and gets in his car. I watch him drive away as Danny thunders back up the stairs.

"He said to give you this." I turn to look at Danny and he's holding my phone in his hand. "Said you left it at home and to call him when you're feeling better."

"Thanks," I say, taking the phone and stuffing it in my pocket. I guess Mateo went into my bedroom because I had to have left it next to my pillow when Danny took me to the ER. Why does he think he's allowed to do that?

"I don't even know what to say. I mean, Jason is bad enough, but you add Mateo Alesci into this and… What the fuck are you thinking?"

I have no good answer for that. I really don't. I don't see the connection between them and I can't even begin to explain my relationship with Mateo, because not one thing we've done can be justified.

"Well, they're both gone now. You wanna hide out here with me tonight?"

"Why are you so nice to me?"

"What?" He laughs.

"Nice to me. You have no good reason to be nice, and yet here you are."

"That's me, Daydreams. The guy who's always there."

"And thank you for the doctor. I'll pay you back somehow."

"No need, OK? I have plenty of money from my job with Phil, and you needed it. That's all there is to it."

His job with Phil. Jason. Mateo. Blood in the driveway if Phil catches Mateo here. What the fuck is going on? But I'm afraid to ask. My life has so few good things in it, I really have no energy to solve this puzzle right now. So I settle on small talk. "I'll still pay you back."

"I'll still be your friend if you don't."

"Friend, huh?"

He walks over to the old leather couch on the wall opposite the bed and sinks down, leaning into the cushions and resting his long muscular arms along the back. "We're friends, right?"

"Yeah, we're friends. But most guys usually want more, you know? Especially when they get invested in a girl."

"Is that what most guys want? I guess I wouldn't know. They don't treat Rocky that way because I'd kick their asses. And if they treat you that way, then you're selling yourself short, Shannon. I'm not most guys and I don't want to pressure you into liking me."

"I do like you."

"I mean, as more than friends."

I sigh.

"I'm not going to kiss you or make a move. It's not my style. You like Mateo?" Danny shrugs. "I can't stop that. Aside from what I think about him personally, I don't think a relationship with a guy that much older than you is gonna work. But I'm only eighteen, so what do I know? It's your life."

"Thanks for that," I say, placing my hand over my still tender ear. "I appreciate all of it, Danny, I really do."

He gets up and grabs the three prescription containers off the side table next to the bed and hands me a water bottle. "You've only taken two doses since last night, and I couldn't get you to roll over for the drops. So take these," he says, shaking out a pill from each of the bottles and handing them over. "And I'll put the drops in while you watch some TV."

I take the pills and gulp them down and then lie on my side with the infected ear up. Danny grabs the drops and sits down next to me, gently moving my hair aside so he can see. "It looks a lot better today." And then he drops the medicine in and I gasp from the cold sting. "Just call me Dr. Dan, the guy who fixes everything."

I smile and close my eyes, enjoying the relief that comes from the drops.

The next time I wake, Danny is snoring on the couch and his face is lit up by the TV. I wonder what he meant by what he thinks of Mateo personally? He's probably known him a long time. Phil must know him too, since Rocky made that remark about blood in the driveway if Phil catches him here.

But I'm not in any condition to think too hard right now. So I eat two more pills and put some more drops in before closing my eyes again, content to sleep it off and let the real world wait me out.

24

I'm wearing Rocky's jeans—which are too long for me, so they scuff on the ground when I walk—and Danny's Metallica t-shirt when I make it to design class and start unpacking my laptop the next morning. No one called my phone, not that I would've answered it, but still. Neither of the two assholes in my life even bothered to call, and while Jason can go fuck himself, Mateo doesn't get a pass like that. Not after our date last Saturday.

Just what the fuck is his deal? He takes me to the beach, introduces me to his family, and then disappears for three days?

No. That's not right.

"Shannon Drake?" Mrs. Sheridan, the teacher, calls from her desk.

"Yeah?"

"Mr. Bowman sent a request for you to see him in his office when you got in. Take the pass with you."

I sigh and push back from my chair as I pack my laptop back up. I take the pass and head out to the main building.

Mr. Bowman is with a student in that giant room they call an office, and he points to a chair, ordering me to sit and wait in front of the attendance lady. I know her, I worked in the office last semester, so she sends me a sympathetic smile.

Ten minutes later Mr. Bowman is ready for me. "Let's take a walk, Shannon," he says, directing me out into the hallway.

I sigh again, like the teen I am, and follow him. He goes right out the front doors and stands at the top of the steps that look out on the traffic on Lincoln Avenue. "Is everything OK?" he asks.

"Yes," I hesitantly say.

"Mr. Portman called and reported that you failed to show up for school last night."

"Who's Mr. Portman?"

"Your science teacher at Gilbert?" he replies, getting a little pissed off. "And you left school early on Tuesday too."

"Oh," I say. "Well, he never told me his name. And I missed class because I was really sick. I have a receipt from the ER. Danny Alexander had to take me in on Tuesday afternoon."

"What about yesterday?" he asks, taking my receipt.

"I was still sick, Mr. Bowman. Look, I have three prescriptions for my ear." I fish out my pills and drops and hold them out. He takes them, frowning at my codeine.

"Did you take this?" And now I can tell he's mad.

"I was in pain, Mr. Bowman. I'm not a fucking addict, OK? Just because my sister OD'd on painkillers doesn't mean I'm abusing them too, you know."

He lets out a long breath. "I'm sorry, I wasn't insinuating—"

"You *were* insinuating," I say, standing my ground. Jesus Christ. I cannot cut a break.

"Well, you can't have them at school, Shannon. If anyone sees these, you'll be suspended. And I don't need to remind you that you cannot afford a suspension if you want to graduate."

"Well, I haven't even been home since I got out of the ER. I stayed at Danny's house. So I won't bring them tomorrow, OK? God."

He stares at me for a few moments and then his expression softens. "How are things going in science then?"

"Great," I say. "I'm like more than halfway done with that stupid class. All the tests are open-book and you can do them at your own pace. I told you I didn't need another science credit. It's a waste of time and resources to make me—"

"Fine, fine. How is... Mr. Alesci?"

"OK, I guess."

"I was told he had to leave town for work?"

"I have no idea. All I know is that I showed up on Monday and he didn't." I'm pissed about that and hell if I'm gonna cover for him when he didn't even bother to tell me not to waste my time and money on the bus.

"It was work-related. There must've been a miscommunication. He called in that morning and said he was in Arizona for his graduate studies."

"Noted," I say.

"Are you going tonight?"

"I guess, if he's going to be there."

"He will." And then Mr. Bowman gives me a long sideways glance. "Is everything OK with trig?"

I shrug.

"Has anything… inappropriate occurred?"

"What?" Fuck. Jesus fuck, fuck, fuck. He knows something.

"The janitor reported that he saw you get on his motorcycle on Friday evening. Did you?"

"Look, it was late and I didn't have any money for the bus so Mateo—"

"Mateo?"

"—Mr. Alesci," I say, ready to kick myself for that slip-up, "offered to give me a ride since I had to walk. And look, I'm not about to turn down a ride in the dark, OK? Sue me for wanting to get home in time to take care of my niece."

He pauses at the mention of Olivia. "How is she?"

"Fine. I have to get back to class, Mr. Bowman. I'm not skipping school, I was sick."

He smiles and I make my getaway. I am really on thin ice with him now, thanks to that ride last week. And that sucks. It sucks all the balls in the world because I don't have any money for the bus today either.

"Danny?"

He's sitting next to me on the wall today at lunch. He's been acting a little big-brother all day. He even bought me a ham and cheese sandwich for lunch so I could wash down my pills and met me at the end of each class so he could walk me to my next one.

"Yeah, Daydreams. I can tell you want something, so just spit it out. You've been acting quiet all day."

"Can you give me a ride to school tonight? I wouldn't ask, but I don't have money for the bus."

He narrows his eyes at me. "Won't you get in trouble from your boyfriend for that?"

I look around to see if anyone is paying attention, but thankfully, they are all involved in their own conversations. "Shhh," I say. "Please."

The lunch bell rings and he hops down off the wall. "You know I will. Pick you up too, if you need it."

"Thank you," I say. And then he grabs my backpack and walks with me to English, where I am thankful that I finished the required book last week because I fall asleep on my desk the minute the boy at the podium starts reading from *The Good Earth*.

25

Mateo is wearing a suit today when I walk into class at five o'clock. "You could've called me back last night."

Oh, he has some nerve. "You could've called me, period," I snap.

"I had to go out of town for—"

"I know," I snap again. "Bowman pulled me aside this morning and drilled me about you. The fucking janitor saw me get on your bike last Friday and apparently that is considered inappropriate."

He taps his mechanical pencil on the desk and then abruptly stands up. "Let's go now. I'll take you home."

"No," I say. "No. I haven't made any progress in this class and I'm going to fail. Give me the tests for units one and two."

"We haven't even gone over the chapters yet."

"Whose fault is that? Give me the tests."

"We had an arrangement."

"Are you kidding me? Bowman is on to us. I'm not getting in trouble because you want your dick sucked."

"Don't," he warns.

"Don't what? Speak the truth?"

"That's not what I was thinking."

"Well, that's what you were thinking last week. Danny is picking me up in forty-five minutes so I can be home to

183

take care of Olivia when Jason goes to work. So stop fucking around and give me the tests."

He sighs and I get a lot of satisfaction out of that sigh. Fuck him and all his stupid rules. All his control-freak shit. All his 'get naked in my kitchen and do your work' orders. Just fuck him.

He opens up his backpack and takes out a folder that says 'Shannon' on the front of it and I have to roll my eyes. He pulls out a sheet of paper and hands it to me. "Test one," he says.

I snatch it out of his hand and go sit down on the other side of the room, glancing at the clock as I try to calm myself. I don't have much time and I really want to get two tests done.

My hope dies the second I read the first question. Problem one has four parts and then ten associated questions. Jesus fucking Christ. My ear is pounding, that's how angry I am.

Label the quadrants, angles, x and y coordinates, and radians of the unit circle. Then answer the questions below using your diagram as a guide.

This will take me an hour at least. I hate math. I get up, throw the test at Mateo, and walk out.

Fuck him. Fuck trig. Fuck this stupid ear.

I text Danny and ask him to pick me up. I'm never going to graduate because I am never going to pass this class. Ever. Memorize the fucking unit circle? Are they kidding me with that shit? Who the fuck needs to memorize the goddamned unit circle? *It's called a computer, you assholes.*

I pull out my cigarettes and only have one left. Figures. I light it up and I'm puffing before I even make it outside. The janitor looks at me, ready to say something as I pass, but I look him straight in the eye and say, "I dare you, asshole. I dare you to talk to me right now. And fuck you for telling Bowman I got a ride home. Just fuck you."

I really want the door to slam behind me, but of course, it's got one of those soft-closing mechanism things on it, and it simply whooshes closed with a small puff of air.

And then opens up again. "Shannon."

"Go away," I tell Mateo. "I'm not even kidding."

"Why are you so mad? I get it, I didn't call. But it was a rush thing, OK? It was a big deal for me. I didn't have time to call, and I told Bowman to send you a message at school so you didn't show up."

"Well, I did show up because that school is stupid. No one ever got me that message and I took the bus all the way over here. I didn't even have enough money left over to eat that day!"

I scream that last part. I might be losing it. All the shit that's happened over the past year is coming out right now and Mateo had better get the hell away from me, because he's my target.

Mateo sighs. "Do you want to go to Hawaii with me for spring break?"

"What?" I snap.

He's got a pathetic smile on his face. Something that might be sheepishness, confusion, or maybe just fear. I hope it's fear. "I have to go to Hawaii over break to do this demonstration of the stuff I'm writing about in my dissertation, and I'd like you to come."

"Why?"

"Because I'm sorry. I should've called you first. And I want you to come. See what I do. Plus, if you spend any more time with Danny Alexander, I will throttle him."

"You will not. He's picking me up right now and if you so much as look at him funny, I will never talk to you again."

Mateo sighs, runs his fingers through his hair, and then walks away and goes back inside.

I told him.

I tap my foot as I smoke.

Yup. Told his ass right off.

I blow some rings.

He can take his Hawaii trip and shove it up his ass.

Ten minutes later my cigarette is long gone and I'm calming down when Danny pulls in to the parking lot. I get in the passenger side and hug my backpack to my chest.

"Bad night?"

I nod.

"Did you fight with him?"

"Yes, a little. But that's not the half of it. I wanted to take a test today to try and make progress in this class, so he gave it to me, and goddammit, Danny, it was the longest fucking question ever."

"So you gave up and walked out?"

"How'd you guess?"

"You're riled up."

"I'm calm now."

"So you didn't understand the question? Maybe Mateo needs to change his teaching methods?"

I can't tell if that's a dig or not, so I assume it's not. "It's not that. I understood the question, but I don't think I know the x and y coordinates of the unit circle from memory. I remember glancing at that section and seeing all this square root shit, and I said, fuck that."

Danny laughs. "I didn't realize 'fuck that' was an option in school. Maybe I've been doing it wrong? Did you study it?"

"Study it? I don't *study*, Danny."

"Oh." He laughs. "Excuse me, Miss Einstein. Most of us dimwits have to study to pass tests."

"I didn't mean it that way. I just mean, usually I can remember enough from homework to get by. But this question was ridiculous, you know?"

"Ah," he says as he drives. He probably thinks I'm emotionally unstable and a snooty bitch on top of it. "You wanna go out to eat with me? I'm buying."

My stomach grumbles, that's how much I want to go out to dinner. "I can't. Jason is waiting for me and I can only guess the next fight will be the best all day."

"Want me to come in with you?"

"No." I sigh. "That will just piss him off more."

"OK," he says, turning into my alley and stopping in front of my patio door. "Want a ride to school tomorrow?"

"I'll walk, but thank you so much." I smile at him. "Really. I think you're my only friend in this stupid town."

"An honor I cherish. I'm just down the street if you need me."

"Thank you," I say, getting out of the car and waving as he drives off.

"I told you not to come home," Jason says from the open patio door.

My anger is back. I hate everyone but Danny right now. "Hey, if that's how you feel, let me grab my clothes and I'm outta here."

I push past him and go inside, glance down at sleeping Olivia in that stupid swing, and go into my room. Jason appears in the doorway, hands on either side of the jamb, blocking me in.

I spy the window and calculate my chances of opening it up and squirming my way through if he comes at me.

Not good.

"What?" I hiss, turning to face him. I find attack mode generally defuses things with men. They are constantly surprised at the amount of venom I can spew from this little five-foot-tall body. "You want to be pissed off because I was sick too? Fuck you."

He watches me shove clothes into my pack until it's bulging so much, I can't pull the top drawstring closed. Then he says, calm as can be, "Put your shit back. I'm sorry I didn't take you to the doctor, OK? I was stressed that day."

"You were drunk that day."

"I'm sorry."

"I've heard that so much lately, I want to puke." My eyes start watering and I do not want to cry in front of this asshole, but those tears just come spilling out. "I hate you," I snarl. "I hate you so much, I dream up ways to get you out of my life forever."

He turns to leave.

"But I'll watch Olivia because I love her more than anything. She's the only thing I have left. So go to work and leave me alone."

"Wish granted, Shannon," he says with his back to me. "Wish granted." A few seconds later the front door opens and closes and I'm right where I belong. Alone.

26

Olivia's eyes are open and she's staring up at me as she sways back and forth in her little swing. I stop it and lift her out, snuggling her to my chest. "Do you want to take a bath tonight, Olivia?"

She blinks at me.

"I never give baths, but I'm sick of seeing you in that swing. And I never get to pick your clothes, and your dad does not have the most fashionable taste."

She doesn't have an opinion on that either.

I grab the little blue plastic thing Jason uses to bath her and have a pang of guilt for being such a bitch to him. He does take care of her.

I fill the tub up with warm water, take Olivia's clothes off, and place her inside it. She blesses me with a small smile and some bunched-up fists.

And it's not like she's a difficult baby or anything, but he's managing. Maybe he did love Jill, but that's a huge character flaw in my mind. What kind of man loves a drug addict? And it's not like he met her before she was a druggie, fell in love, and decided to stick by her in bad times. No, that bitch was a two-timing whore. I know I should not speak of my sister like that, but it's the truth. She was cheating on her last boyfriend with Jason, and Jason knew about that.

So what kind of guy picks a girl like her? And how come stupid girls like her always get picked by guys who want to marry them, and I get drug dealers and teachers with inappropriate sexual fantasies?

I breathe deeply as I stew in my anger and then Olivia changes everything when she smiles at me. "I'm sorry, baby. I'm not a very good aunt to you, am I?"

I wash Olivia with a tiny pink washcloth and then run the water again so I can rinse her off. By the time I'm done she's so sleepy, she can barely keep her eyes open. So I dress her in a little peach-colored baby pajama set and place her in the crib in Jason's room.

I walk back out into the living room and scream. "Jesus Christ, Mateo! What the fuck are you doing in here?"

He's standing in my kitchen with a brown paper bag that smells better than it has a right to. "Feeding you. Since you left me with that guilt trip about using your money for bus fare and blah fucking blah about Danny motherfucking Alexander."

"Get out," I say, pointing to the patio slider. I want that food so bad, but no. He's not going to barge his way into my life anymore. Fuck that.

"No," he says, placing the bag on the counter and getting out two plates.

"Mateo." I point up at him now, furious and still shaking from the shock. "Get—"

"No," he growls louder. "Just calm the fuck down and tell me what happened."

"I told you what happened."

"About the part where you had to go to the ER, Shannon."

"Like you care." I fold my arms across my chest.

"Obviously," he says with a heavy sigh. "I care. Or why the hell would I be here?"

"Who knows? You have some sick fascination with young girls? You want to fuck me. You don't want Danny to fuck me." His eye twitches at that remark and I get a little bolder. "You like power, or making teenagers suck your dick in a classroom. You—"

He takes two steps towards me and crosses the safe distance between us, making me move back. But he catches me by the arm and pulls me close to him. "You can say all those things because you're mad, I don't care. But if you *believe* all those things, we have a serious problem."

"Why shouldn't I believe those things?"

"Because I like you, Shannon. I'm here. I'm sorry. I said I was sorry. I'll make it up to you. And you're going to forgive me, because you know I'm telling the truth."

"I don't know that, actually."

He sighs again, and then he twirls me around, pushes me towards the counter, and presses me against it so I'm looking out the window over the kitchen sink. His breath is coming out in long draws, tickling the skin on the back of my neck. And each time it does, his chest presses against my back. His fingers snake up underneath my shirt, and he grabs the cup of my bra and yanks it down, making my nipple spill out into his palm.

He squeezes.

Fuck.

"Give me your left hand," he whispers into my neck.

Now what is he up to? I want to ask, but he'll just give me one of those exasperated sighs, and bark, *Shannon. Do what you're told.* So I hold out my left hand, palm up, and he lets go of my breast so he can wrap his arms all the way around me and take my hand in his.

"Pay attention," he says. And then he uses his finger to draw on the palm of my hand. "What did I just write?"

Really? He wants to play games?

"Answer me, dammit."

"I don't know," I snap. "Do it again."

He does it again and this time his touch tickles my palm so bad, I can feel it tingle long after he stops. "What did I write?"

I take a breath, but my eyes close. Why does he make me feel this way?

"Shannon," he barks. "Fucking answer me."

"The square root of two over two," I say.

"Why did I write that?"

"It's those stupid coordinates on the unit circle test that I didn't know."

"God, sometimes I think you're deaf. Because if you're not deaf, then I have to wonder why you deliberately refuse to listen to me. *Why* did I write that?"

"Dick," I say. "Because you're gonna tell me something about it."

His hand steals back inside my shirt and palms my breast again. "Good girl. Finally you're paying attention. It's a trick, Shannon. A game to help you remember the x and y coordinates. You told me the first day we met your memory is what makes you smart. Unlike you, I listen to the things you tell me, so I came up with a plan to use your talent to help you pass trig. And if you had let me show it to you earlier instead of insisting on taking a test you were so clearly not ready for, you'd be in a better mood right now, I guarantee it."

I sigh.

"Look at your hand."

I glance down.

"If your left hand is the upper right quadrant of the unit circle, and your fingers represent the angles of the unit circle, and your pinky is zero degrees, what's the angle measure of the finger where I'll put your wedding ring one day?"

"You did not just say that."

"Answer me."

"Thirty degrees."

I can feel him smile into my neck and I have to take a deep breath at that.

"What's the finger you use to flip me off?"

"Forty-five degrees."

"And the one you point at me when you're pissed?"

"Sixty degrees."

"Thumb?"

"Ninety."

"Who says you're not smart? You memorized those OK, right?"

"Fourth graders probably know that much, Mateo. I don't need a pep talk."

"Now listen carefully, because what I'm going to show you is magic."

"You're so stupid."

"What did I write on your palm?"

"The square root of two over two."

"OK, now forget about the twos. There's a square root sign and a fraction line. Here's how to remember the coordinates of the unit circle just by looking at your left hand and knowing which angle each finger represents…"

So he tells me.

And he's right. It's memory magic. I will never forget this trick as long as I live, that's how simple it is.

"So when you show up in my kitchen tomorrow to take that test, just remember what I showed you. Now tell me what happened that you needed to go to the ER."

I tell him. I watch his reflection in the window as I talk. I don't know if he knows I can see him, because he never glances back at me. But I can tell that he's sorry he wasn't there when I needed help, because the frown on his face grows longer and longer as the story goes on.

"I'm sorry. Is it better now?" he asks, lifting my hair aside to look at my ear.

"It's better," I say. "I get them all the time and I usually I can just use the leftover drops from the last time to stop it from getting that bad. But I guess my drops were expired and they didn't work."

"OK." He sighs like he's satisfied with my story. I'm not sure how to take that, but he doesn't give me much time to wonder about it, because he says, "Be at my house tomorrow after school, and be ready to make good on our deal."

He starts to back away from me, but I grab his arm and hold him there. "I think we should start over, Mateo. If you really do like me, then let's just start over and try this all again."

His face screws up. "We're not starting over, Shannon. I didn't do all this fun shit just to wipe the slate clean and pretend it didn't happen. You come to my house, you take your clothes off, you study at my kitchen table naked, you suck my dick, you take the test, and if you get one right, I'll lick your pussy until you come. If you pass that test tomorrow, Shannon, I'll fuck your brains out and you will forget all about starting over because what I will do to your body will be so addictive, you will never want me to stop. Do you understand?"

Why did I ever think he'd give in to me? Why did I ever think I had the power in this relationship? He mows me over like a steamroller.

"Do you. Under. Stand?"

"Got it," I say.

"You know, there's something to be said for the wisdom of experience. That's a lesson you need to learn. Now eat your dinner and go to bed. I'll see you tomorrow."

I watch him as he turns and walks to the slider and pulls it open. But he stops again and looks me in the eyes. "And you're coming to Hawaii with me. So just accept it. And let that fuck of a brother-in-law know you won't be babysitting that week."

27

"Triangles are your friend," Mateo says the next day as I wait on his stoop at the back door. He's standing on the other side of the screen, shirtless, and looking like a fucking monster of muscle and masculinity.

"Just let me in," I say.

"They have all the answers, Shannon."

"It's fucking raining, Mateo. Just let me in."

"And if you know certain things about your triangle, you can find out missing information."

I sigh. "Got it. Let me in or I'm going home. I'm all fucking wet."

"You know when triangles are not your friend?"

"Tell me." I give up. He's musing. I have come to the conclusion that Mateo is one of those deep people. People who think too fucking much. I'm not a thinker, I go on instincts. And right now, my instincts are begging me to just tell him what he wants to hear.

"When you're in a relationship."

"Are we in a relationship?" I roll my eyes.

"We are, and I don't want to be part of a love triangle. I let that Danny Alexander thing drop because you needed help and he was there when I wasn't. But I won't make that mistake again. I got us two first-class tickets to Hawaii for spring break."

"Fancy," I say. I hate flying, especially over the ocean. It freaks me out and no amount of posh first-class bullshit will change that.

"You may come in." He opens the screen door wide for me and I step past him.

"I hope you have a fucking dryer," I say, peeling off my clothes. I'm getting fucked today. That's all I'm saying. I've been studying that little unit-circle trick all damn day. I practiced it in art while I was messing around with Photoshop making graphics for my website. I practiced it in PE when I was walking my laps. I practiced it in every class today. I even recited the angles and the radians to myself on the way over here. I'm ready for that test and I am getting fucked.

I drop my clothes on the floor as I make my way to the kitchen and then stand there naked. "Where's the test?"

"Sit," he says, smiling like a fool.

"Mateo—"

"Sit," he growls.

I sigh, but I sit.

"Today you're going to learn how to memorize the trigonometric functions."

"Oh, no, I'm not! Today I'm sucking your dick, taking a test, getting my pussy licked, and then you're fucking me."

He almost laughs. Almost. "No, you're working first."

"That was not the deal."

"I make all the deals, Shannon." He takes my little red textbook out of my backpack and opens it up to chapter two. "I'm surprised you haven't figured that out yet. Now look here…"

An hour later I'm still looking at that damn book, and I've got those functions memorized using his newest trick, but I'm tired now. My eyes are drooping and I'm not even horny anymore. "You're not as fun as you first appeared," I say, yawning.

He eases himself up on the counter of the island in the center of the kitchen and starts unbuckling his belt.

I get a little more interested.

He unbuttons and unzips, looking at me the whole time.

I smile.

He positively grins. "You did good. And you're gonna take the first test, so you get to suck my dick until I come down your throat. But just so we're clear, if you want to take a test tomorrow, you have to suck me at school."

Jesus. Why does he say these things to me? It fucking gets me crazy. I know I should be horrified, but I'm not. He's turning me on. He's turning me into a freak. "Noted."

"Take me out."

I smile so big my cheeks might crack. The last time I gave him a blow job here, I got so bothered by it, I came. Jesus. I ease up out of my seat and walk over to him. His eyes never leave mine. It's like he's more interested in what I'm thinking than my naked body. And that turns me on even more than his hulking cock under those jeans.

I reach for his boxer briefs and pull them down until I see the tip of his cock. God, he has a beautiful cock. The head is thick and perfect. I lick my lips and look up at him.

"Go ahead. If you're so eager, just do it."

I pull him out all the way, pumping him gently in my hand. His hand clamps over mine, squeezing. Making me squeeze harder. I lower my head into his lap and wrap my lips around him, sucking on his tip and then swirling my tongue around it like I'm licking a lollipop. His fingers dig into my hair and urge me to take more of him. I know he likes that deep stuff, and I'm not that good at it. But I try hard. I try my best to please him and I'm rewarded with a moan.

I moan too, my vocal cords humming against his shaft as he presses down on my head. I decide to just go for it. Fuck everything. I forget about everything but him. I take him in as far as I can, gag, pull back, the saliva spilling out of my mouth. But I dive down for more and this makes him pull my head away. He jumps down off the counter and stands in front of me.

"Kneel and put your hands on my thighs, Shannon. And don't move them."

It's not an order. Not something I must obey. But the way he says it—well, it makes me *want* to obey. I place my hands flat against his muscular thighs as he gathers my hair in a ponytail, gripping it so tight, it pulls on my scalp.

"Look at me," he says.

I do. I want nothing more than to look at him. His jaw is covered with stubble two days old. His green eyes are at half-mast as he gazes down at me. His dick is hard and right in front of my lips.

"Open," he says. "I'm gonna fuck your face and come down your throat."

I open my mouth and he shoves himself inside so fast, his cock bumps up against my soft palate and makes me gag. But he doesn't wait for me this time. He's in control. He's the one with the power. He pulls my head back by my hair and then thrusts me forward again, hitting that same spot. My fingers are clenched around the loose denim of his jeans as I force myself to give in to what he wants from me.

I never stop looking at him. My eyes are only on him.

"Fuck, you're beautiful." And the he rams his cock again and again. I gag, and spit, and noises are coming from my throat that I've never heard before. But each time he thrusts, he moans.

I am doing it right, that's what those moans mean.

The next time he hits my soft palate I wrap my lips around him tighter and suck, bobbing my head to his rhythm. Back and forth so fast, he loses control, stiffens, and then his warm semen is spilling down my throat.

"Swallow," he groans. "Swallow me."

I swallow every single drop and when he pulls away and the saliva is spilling down my chin, I lean forward and lick his tip.

"I fucking love you," he says.

I—can't move. I can't speak. I have tears from the stress of being face-fucked running down my cheeks and I'm sure my eye makeup is all smeared. I must look horrible.

But he just said he loves me.

"I do, Shannon. I knew the first time I saw you, I was going to love you forever. It was one of those things you just know."

And then he pulls me to my feet and kisses me on the mouth. A long, deep kiss that says more than his words ever will.

He loves me. I can feel it in my core.

He takes my hand and leads me through the kitchen, past the living room, and into the hallway where I've never been before. We stop in his bedroom and he kicks off his boots and drops his pants. He takes my hand again and leads me over to his bed and then he lies down and says, "Rub your pussy over my mouth."

Fuck. This dirty talk does me in. I gulp some air and then climb onto the bed, straddling his waist and bracing myself with my palms flat on his hard chest.

"Go on, do it," he encourages me.

I scoot up his body until my knees are resting on the bed on either side of his head. And then I lower myself down.

His tongue reaches up and flicks against my clit.

Oh, God. I might die of pleasure. Is it possible to die of pleasure?

My hips start moving back and forth, his scratchy chin rubbing my tender folds in all the right ways. His tongue darts in and out of my pussy. He reaches up and squeezes my breasts, and then he pinches my nipples so hard, I have to let out a squeal. He releases them, but smacks the cheek of my ass.

He stops my hips for a moment and looks up at me. I'm mesmerized by his eyes. "Fuck my face like I did yours. And when you come, I'll flip you over and show you what a good time really feels like."

I brace my hands on the head board, my knees trembling from keeping myself positioned over the top of him. And then I do exactly what he wants.

I fuck him. I rub myself all over his chin. His tongue does a dance that I will never understand, but I don't need to. It's not a mathematical mystery that requires solving. It's nothing but pure ecstasy.

And when I come, I come hard. My head falls back as he laps me up. And then he does exactly what he promised. He flips us over and enters me from the top. His palms cradle my cheeks. His mouth kisses my mouth. And we go slow. We look at each other—gaze at each other—as the pleasure builds to something close to infinity.

We come together in every way possible.

It's moaning, and writhing, and grunting. It's sex.

But it feels like love.

I might never have understood what that word meant before, but I do now.

Mateo is love.

We lie there afterward, him mostly talking about what we will do in Hawaii, me still focused on the mind-blowing sex. And then it starts to get dark and I know I need to go home. He helps me dress and walks me across the street, kissing me goodbye on the other side of my patio gate, my head spinning from the leftover lust and the loud hum of the 5 freeway.

I'm addicted to him and what he does to my body. There's no starting over or going back now. I am just addicted and I need more.

I walk inside and drift around the apartment, ignoring Jason's bad mood as he gathers his stuff to leave for work. And I realize that I never did take my test today.

28

Mateo and I settle into a routine after that. I see him every day but Sunday. The science class at Gilbert finishes up mid-February when all my open-book tests for that semester are turned in and I take the C as a grade. So I stop going to Gilbert altogether. Mateo arranges for us to meet in the library at Anaheim on Tuesdays and Thursdays, and even though this is far less fun because we agreed that sexy times are out of the question with Bowman so close, it's far easier for me to not have to take the bus anymore.

The rest of the days we meet at his house and do the whole naked tutoring, dick-sucking, pussy-licking, test-taking thing. I don't know where he gets his problems from. I think he actually makes them up special for me because every one of them has to do with astronomy and he says each of the answers are something he needs for his dissertation project.

I highly doubt that, but I humor him and solve them after we go over examples.

On Saturdays he takes me on a date and it's never the same place twice. He took me to the planetarium in LA where he said he sorta works. Who knew? Not me. But I guess his dissertation isn't on stars at all. Not really. It's on the educational value of laser shows to generate interest in astronomy and math in young people. He didn't have a show ready for me that day, that's why we're going to

Hawaii, he said. That's the first time anyone will see his project and he needs to gather data for his dissertation defense. I guess he's been traveling for the past year trying to garner support from universities and organizations who use a planetarium as part of their astronomy program and that's why he was in Arizona when I got sick.

Overachieving nerd. With star tattoos. And a hard body. And a big cock. And that fucking chin. Oh. My. God.

I'm falling for him.

No, I take that back. I'm on the goddamned ground banging my head against a rock, because if everything goes well on our trip to Hawaii this week, he'll be traveling a lot doing much the same thing after he defends his dissertation.

I sigh as I sit on the back steps waiting for him to pick me up for the airport. He's late. We leave in four hours and LAX is a good hour-and-a-half drive in traffic at this time of day.

A horn honks in the driveway, and I get up off the stoop and peek around the corner of the house. Oh, shit. It's his mother in a pale yellow, classic Mercedes roadster. She's got the top up and she's leaning out the window. "Shannon, honey. Mateo is running late and he asked me to run you to the airport."

"Oh," I say, disappointed.

"Come on. Do you need help with your bags?"

"No," I say, grabbing my backpack from the stairs and walking to the passenger side door. I slide in, my bare legs loving the softness of the leather interior.

"He didn't buy you a bag for this trip?" she asks, looking at my pack. "What kind of animal did I raise?"

I giggle at that. "He did offer. He was just as appalled as you that I was taking a ten-dollar backpack to Hawaii. But I said no. I'm not a traveler. I probably wouldn't get a lot of use out of it."

She gives me a sideways glance as we back out of the driveway and get on Broadway. "Honey, Mateo loves to travel, so you should just take him up on that offer. You're going to need it."

"Hmmm," I say.

"What's that mean?"

I like Gigi. I've seen her regularly since Mateo first introduced us. Mostly when we go eat at Alesci's Laguna. But she's been in Alesci's Anaheim a few times when we've stopped in too. We eat there once a week at least. "I don't know. I can't predict the future. And Olivia is here. I can't just go on trips all the time, you know? Jason was pissed off about this week, but I told him months ago, so there was nothing he could do."

"I see," she says, getting on the 5 north. "But they are not your only family, Shannon."

"No, they really are. I know it's hard to understand that, coming from such a big one yourself, but—"

"No, sweetie. We're your family now too."

I think I blush. I have no idea what to say to that. Does she really think Mateo and I will be together after he finishes his dissertation? Because I'm not that delusional.

"What are you going to do after graduation, Shannon?"

"Oh, I'm thinking about web design. I'm doing a project in school right now and I really like it. Plus, I can do graphic design at the same time. It's sort of a win-win for me."

"Do you do web design? I didn't know that. Would you like to redesign the Alesci's site?"

"Oh, wow, that must be a huge project."

"Well, we can start small, maybe? How about just the Anaheim site? And then we'll see where we are when you're done with that."

"Yeah," I say, excited. Gigi speeds up to get over, and then we get stuck in bumper-to-bumper traffic trying to merge onto the 91. "I'd really like that, actually."

"I'll pay you, of course. What do websites go for these days? Last time we redid it I think it was somewhere in the neighborhood of eight thousand dollars."

"What?" I almost choke. "I'm pretty sure my services aren't worth eight thousand dollars, Gigi."

"Honey," she says, raising an eyebrow. "Never undersell yourself. Always know your worth. And if you come out high, you can always lower your price during negotiations. But since I came in low, as a new businesswoman you will want to counter with something higher. Include a list of your talents and services. Now what are you worth?"

Is she asking me to raise the price on her?

"Shannon?"

"Yeah, OK." I take a few seconds to collect my thoughts. "Well, I'll do an original design that will showcase the history of the Anaheim store. Include some of those old photos you have hanging on the walls. And pictures of the family who work there, of course." Lots of cousins work at the Anaheim store. "And you know what, Gigi? You know what you can maybe add in?" I get a little excited at this idea.

"Tell me, honey." She's smiling big at my enthusiasm.

"An online order form for delivery."

"You're a genius, Shannon."

"Right?" I laugh. "People can pay online and stuff. Then the food just appears at their door. We can totally set that up. I'm pretty sure they have some kind of extension I could buy that will have the basics."

"I love it," she says.

"But I might need to hire a programmer for the custom stuff. I'm not sure I could do it all myself."

"So true, honey. OK, you drive a hard bargain, but you're right. You need ten thousand for that site. Deal."

Ten thousand dollars. I'm speechless.

But I realize she's offering me her hand to shake on the deal and I take it, leaning back into the soft leather seats, smiling. "Thank you," I say. "I know you're going out of your way to help me and I just want you to know, I really appreciate it."

"You're family, Shannon. That's what families do for each other. And if," she gives me a sideways glance, "you and Mateo have a disagreement, well, the job is not conditional on your relationship with him. Put a plan together and bring it to me the next time you're in Laguna, Ok, sweetie?'"

"Wow, OK. Thank you, Gigi. You have no idea how much I needed a break like this."

"I have an idea." She smiles to herself as we drive. "But family takes care of each other. That's how we do and that's how it should be."

I bask in the glow of that little revelation and let myself daydream about Mateo. Could we really be together after all this school stuff is over? I have not thought about it. Not because I don't want it, but because it just didn't seem possible that he felt that way about me. He cracks jokes about serious things. And this whole Hawaii trip is kind of a big deal. But he said he didn't want me home alone all week with Danny Alexander ready to swoop in and take his place.

Danny's not like that though. We're just friends. But Matco is still possessive.

Gigi talks the rest of the drive and I mostly listen, lost in my own thoughts. Mateo is waiting for me at United arrivals curbside check-in when we pull up and he opens my door for me.

"Have fun, kids!" Gigi calls, as Mateo takes my backpack.

We wave as she drives off. "Sorry I didn't pick you up myself. Last-minute details." He takes in a big breath like he had a stressful day.

"You're all ready now?" I ask.

"I think so."

"Nervous?" I've never seen Mateo nervous.

"Little bit," he says, ushering me to the porter at baggage. "You want to check that bag?"

"Sure," I say.

He checks me in and we get our boarding passes, then proceed through security and make our way to our gate. By that time they're already boarding the first-class passengers, so we get right in line and find our seats.

"Fancy," I tell him, as the attendant serves us drinks and starts asking us to choose a meal off the dinner menu.

"Nothing but the best for you."

"Speaking of the best… your mother's car?"

"Don't even get me started. That thing is worth a hundred and sixty thousand dollars and she drives it around like it's a station wagon. I want to strangle her every single time she pulls up in it."

"She must love it."

"She does," he says softly. "My dad gave it to her when they first met."

"Awww."

"He died five years ago and I think she drives it because it reminds her of their love."

"Double awww." I have to place my hand over my heart. "I love your mom."

"She likes you too."

"She hired me to redesign the Anaheim website."

"I like web design as your career choice. You can do it from anywhere."

"Will I need to do it from anywhere?"

"We won't know until I'm done with my defense, I guess."

We. God, maybe Gigi was right? Maybe he's really planning on us being together after this is over?

"I've got a lot of institutions interested in my project, but no buyers yet. Hopefully that will change tomorrow." He's holding my hand and he brings it to his lips and kisses it. And then he gives me a sheepish smile that is so different from the man who usually has me sucking his dick in his kitchen while talking triangles.

"You're gonna do great," I say. "You're gonna wow the fuck out of those Hawaiian nerds."

His face lights up with amusement. "That's why I love you, Shannon. You always know how to make things right."

"Aww. You're a romantic like your dad." I giggle.

"I did learn from the best." He leans over and kisses my lips. It's one of those long, slow ones. He doesn't break away until he's good and finished, even when the attendant stands there asking for our empty drink cups so we can take off. "I know how to treat a woman, Shannon. So far we've done the 'getting to know you' stuff, but the 'we're in it together' stuff is yet to come. So get ready."

I stare at him, my mouth probably hanging open. "I'm ready."

"Finally." He chuckles and hands our empty cups to the waiting attendant.

29

He wasn't kidding. He does know how to treat a woman. There's a chauffeur waiting for us in Hilo after we get our bags and the whole drive to the hotel, I am jittery with anticipation. The closer we get to the ocean, the more I realize that this is not just a trip. This is a milestone in our relationship.

The Four Seasons Hotel in Kailua-Kona is a long drive. An hour and a half from the astronomy center. And if that little fact wasn't enough to convince me this trip is about us, then the romantic ocean-front room is. Mateo tips the bell boy as I stand out on the terrace. Waves are crashing not fifty feet from me. The beach looks perfect, and the sun is just about to rise, so it lights up the west with a haze of pink and orange. I know we have a big day, but I can't stop myself.

As soon as the bell boy leaves I turn to Mateo. "We need to swim! Now!"

He laughs. "You act like you've never seen a beach before."

"I don't even know what to say about this, Mateo. Really, I had no idea you had this kind of money."

He comes up behind me and wraps his arms around me. "Does it bother you?"

"Are you kidding?" I giggle. "No. But I know this is special. I won't expect this kind of luxury every time we go somewhere."

"Why not?" he asks. "That's what money is for."

"Because I'm young. I haven't worked for it. I should have to put in a little more effort to get things like this."

"You can put more effort in any time you want, Miss Drake. But I'm not keeping track. You'd really rather swim than sleep with me right now?"

We're all off schedule. We slept on the plane, since that was a six-hour ride. But we got in at three am and it took forever to get here and get checked in, so now it's closer to six. He needs to be at the planetarium at noon to start setting up and that's all the way back by the airport, so sleep is probably the better option.

And of course, who in their right mind would choose swimming over sleeping with a man like Mateo?

"I choose you," I say, turning into him and leaning up on my tiptoes to kiss him on the mouth.

"Right answer," he says, taking me by the hand and leading me towards the bed.

Six hours later we're dressed—Mateo is wearing a dark blue suit and I'm in a semi-wrinkled sundress—and messing around with his computer in the planetarium control room.

"How old are the kids?" I ask Mateo, who is kneeling down trying to figure out how to hook up his computer. I have figured out from conversation that Mateo has written software for this presentation. Some kind of very impressive software. I'm not overly surprised because he's a genius.

"Twelve," he says. "Sixth graders. That's the optimal age to get them interested enough in science to plan a high-school math curriculum."

"Ah. I see I'm six years too late."

He looks up at me and shoots me a scowl. "Don't, OK?"

"Don't what?"

"Make jokes about your age. It bugs me."

"Why?" I say, kneeling down to grab the cord he's not seeing, but needs.

"Because it's always been an issue for you and I don't want it to be an issue today. There are a lot of important people here from other planetariums around the world I'm counting on being impressed. I really don't want to be wondering if you think I'm too old for you." He takes the cord from my hand and slides it into the port on the top of the control panel. There's a ton of doohickeys and knobs, things I have no clue about, but which look very serious.

"OK," I say. "And it's not really an issue."

"Good," he says, his smile back. "Because I have a surprise for you."

I give him a sideways look and an eyebrow arch for good measure. "Should I be worried about that surprise?"

"No." He laughs and gives me a kiss.

The doors open below and kids start filing in. The control room is situated up above the seats, much like a projector is in a movie theatre.

"OK," he says, "go find your seat. And here." He grabs a program off the console and hands it to me. "You can read this while you wait. I'll be down in"—he checks his watch—"fifteen minutes."

He starts to turn away but I place my hands on each of his shoulders and make him go still. "You're going to do great, Mr. Alesci. You are the smartest man I've ever met. You will rock this place so hard, they won't know what hit them."

He lets out a deep breath as I straighten his tie and lean up on my tiptoes to give him a kiss on the cheek. "Thank you, Shannon. I needed that." He gives me another quick kiss just as the director of the planetarium comes in and they start to chat.

I take my cue and leave, making my way down the stairs. It's sorta interesting what Mateo does. Astronomy. Very unusual, especially for a such a tough guy. I do love the stars on his body though. I trace them every time we make love at his house. Some of them are patterns. I guess those are constellations. I'm not all that up on my astronomy, but I have a feeling he's going to wow me today. Especially if what he's working on is suitable for twelve-year-olds.

I chuckle to myself at that, and then start searching for my seat as I walk into the auditorium through a special side door. It's not hard to find, I'm in seat A-15. Right smack in front of the podium.

I take a seat next to a girl who is diligently reading her program. She has dark pigtails that hang halfway down her back and she's wearing white shorts and a yellow top that make her bronze skin glow. "What's this word?" she asks me, shoving her unruly friend away in the seat next to her.

I lean over and find the words she's having trouble with. "Trigonometry," I say.

"What's that?" She crinkles her nose.

"It's math. You use circles and triangles to figure out mysteries of the universe."

"Do not!" the hyper girl in the next seat says.

"Be quiet, Kani," the pigtailed girl snaps, before turning her attention back to me. "How do you do that?"

"Um…" Shit, I should have an answer. I feel inadequate as Mateo's biggest cheerleader. "Well, the guy who is talking today is my boyfriend and he knows all about it. So if you listen to what he says, you'll understand when you leave here."

"Does he study the planets?"

"Ahhh…" Damn. I should know this. "He studies stars. And… exoplanets. Those are planets that orbit around stars that are very far away from our sun." I feel proud that I actually remember that. Mateo has been reading about exoplanets all semester.

"I think I like stars."

"Mmm," I say, my eyes wandering to the picture of Mateo in her program. He's got his dress shirt sleeves rolled up in that picture and I can see his tattoos. "Me too."

The lights dim and Mateo comes out of the special door that leads to the control room, and then all the kids start shushing each other to be quiet.

"Good afternoon," he starts, his eyes finding me immediately. I smile at him. Beam at him, actually. I've never really seen Mateo in his work mode. He's all smart and sexy-looking right now.

He introduces himself and tells the kids a little bit about his project, why he's here, and what they can expect. And then the place goes complete black and every kid gasps.

But then the ceiling lights up with stars and begins to move. It swirls, slowly at first, making the stars begin to blur, and then faster and faster until the kids are squealing and the stars are so blurred, they form white circles above out heads.

It stops, and Mateo talks. And with each thing he describes, the show above us changes. We move past the Solar System and he zooms in on a faraway smear of bright colors, calling it by name.

And when I look around, every head is turned up. Every mouth is open in awe. And every set of eyes is filled with wonder.

Mateo has that effect on me as well.

He talks about the stars for a long time. He talks about faraway planets that we can't actually see, but he's got animations that capture everyone's attention and make them all go, "Ohhhh."

God, I might love this man for real.

And then he brings us all back to Earth and lights the ceiling up with the outlines of the constellations. "The ancients came up with these pictures," Mateo says. "But you can come up with your own pictures in the stars. Should we make a new one today?"

"Yes!" they all scream.

"OK," he says, clicking the remote in his hand. "But we have to solve problems to do it. So who knows the answer to this problem?"

It's an easy multiplication problem, so they all shout it out. And up above us, a line appears. It connects one star to the next. He calls out another problem, and another, and each time the lines connect the stars like a dot-to-dot puzzle.

"He's spelling something," rowdy Kani whispers from the other side of pigtail girl.

"It's a name," my new friend whispers back.

It *is* a name. My name.

"Are there any Shannons in here?" Mateo asks once it's all spelled out.

Everyone looks around, searching for Shannon.

"Come on, someone here is named Shannon." He looks right at me. I shake my head, so embarrassed. "You?" he calls out to me. "Your name is Shannon?" He holds out his hand. "Come here, Shannon." And he says it in that growly voice he usually reserves for our kitchen antics.

The girls next to me squeal and the pigtailed one starts pushing me to join him up front.

"Oh, my God." But I get up and walk over to him, taking his hand.

"This is my girlfriend," he says, looking at me with the biggest grin. "And I tricked her into coming to see this show today so I could ask her something."

Everyone gasps.

"You are not doing this," I whisper, my back to the crowd.

"I am," he whispers back, then raises his voice. "She's the smartest girl in here, but she doesn't think she is."

Kids start calling out sweet things about my brain and I almost double over in laughter.

"I've been tricking her for months now. Making her solve problems so that when I asked her this question, I could trace her solutions in the stars and get the answer I wanted."

Snickers.

"So, Shannon Drake, here's my question." I roll my eyes. I know he's not going to ask me to marry him, that is ridiculous. I'm eighteen years old. "What do you think about me so far?" He winks. "Should we see what Shannon's answer is in the stars?"

"Yes!" they all call out.

He hands me the little clicker he's using to start each animation. "Be my guest," he says. "I can't wait to see what you have to say."

Jesus Christ. I have never smiled so much in my life.

I click through the animations, one at a time. Slowly at first, but the kids urge me to go faster to see what it says.

They call it after a few letters.

"I love you," I say, when the presentation is complete.

"I never doubted you, babe." He's grinning so wide, so proud of himself. And the kids are going crazy with excitement. "Thank you for coming, everyone, and there's lots of puzzles for you to solve in your programs today, so make sure you go home and figure them all out. Now let me ask you one more question."

He waits as they settle.

"Do I make science and math fun or what?"

A chorus of screaming yeses.

Wildly successful presentation over.

It's only then that I notice a large group of people dressed in suits in the back of the room. They are smiling and clapping for Mateo as he takes my hand and raises it up with his in triumph.

They are the representatives, I realize. From other planetariums around the world. People he's counting on to buy his new educational software. His very expensive educational product that came from the fruit of all his years of hard work and research.

And they are sold.

I fuck the shit out of Mateo Alesci that night on the beach outside our room. I fuck the shit out of him every night we spend there. And every morning. And during our afternoon naps. I cannot get enough of him.

I do love him. And I never want this to end.

"Stop it," I say, pushing Mateo off me. "I'm working, dammit."

He bites my shoulder and I can't help but smile. "School's out."

"Not until next week. I need to finish this assignment."

"The only assignments that matter are mine," he growls, taking his nibbles to my earlobe.

I shake my head and try not to giggle. "Not true. Your mother is expecting mad skills for her website and I'm not even done with my own site yet."

"Play with me, Shannon," he whines. "Please. I'll let you suck my cock."

I look at him from the corner of my eye. "Behave now and I'll let you spank me later."

His gaze goes all drifty as he pictures it. He likes to play Bad Little Schoolgirl with me. He has a paddle with my name on it and everything.

I can only roll my eyes. But I'm more than willing to put on knee socks and a tartan skirt and let him bend my bare ass over his lap.

He hits hard too. He leaves red palm prints on my cheeks and then he takes a picture of them so I can see when we're done. But just picturing myself spread open for his inspection, my long hair dangling down his legs, my hands grabbing on to his suit pants...

Jesus. I close my laptop and say, "What do you have in mind?"

"Hmmmm," he moans, letting his hands explore my body. They leave my shoulders and grab my breasts. I'm already naked because it's a kitchen work day. "I want the whole neighborhood to hear us," he whispers. "Everyone. I want to fuck you in the front yard."

"Oh, no," I say. I don't tell him no often, but no. "I'm not having sex in your front yard." I might be sitting naked in his kitchen, but I have to draw the line somewhere. Plus, the blinds are closed and it's late. So no one is looking in here.

"No?" he says, taking my hand and pulling me up from my seat.

"No," I say, but I'm already smiling because he's sucking on my nipple and there's no chance he's not getting his way. I might *say* no, but it never works. Mateo always gets his way.

"I want everyone to know, Shannon," he says, taking his kisses up to my shoulder again. "I'm tired of hiding you in here."

"We're not hiding." Not really. We stopped hiding after Hawaii. But there's nothing to hide anyway. I finished my last trig test two weeks ago and Mateo turned in my grade. Even Mr. Bowman couldn't stop us now.

"I want to flaunt you. Make you come so hard, everyone within two blocks hears you scream my name. But I want to do it my way." He reaches into his pocket and pulls out a yellow silk scarf.

"Really?" I ask. "I mean, I get the whole blindfold thing, but yellow? It's probably see-through."

"Let me put it on you and find out."

I throw up my hands, unimpressed. Mateo's ten years on me have not gone unnoticed. He's got a lot more experience than I do in the sexual imagination department. "Give it your best shot, cowboy."

He chuckles as he places the soft silk over my eyes and ties it tight at the back of my head. "Now follow me."

"Wait, we're not going outside."

"Define outside."

"Mateo—"

"Shannon—"

"I don't want to fuck in the front yard."

"You do," he whispers, biting my ear again. "Trust me."

When he says trust me he really means it. It's not a flippant joke or something casual. He's serious. He's asked me to trust him a lot over the past few months. "Fine." I give in. I always give in.

He takes my hand again and leads me forward, flipping out all the lights in the house as we pass through rooms. The scarf is see-through, but only when the lights are on. So by the time we make our way to the front of the house, I can't see shit. It's got to be past eleven at night right now, and the porch light isn't on when we cross over the threshold, him giving me a little warning about the lip of wood trim that separates the house from the porch.

"Does this excite you?" I ask. "Fucking me on the porch in the dark?"

"Should I turn the lights on?"

"No." I laugh.

"Then don't jump to conclusions about what we're doing."

I bite my lip, nervous. What did I agree to this time?

"Stand right here."

I take a deep breath and let it out as I listen to the creak of the screen door on the porch. "Mateo?"

"Don't move," he orders me. But he's not on the porch, he's out in the yard. And the screen door is still open because I never heard it slam shut.

"What are you doing?" I whisper. But he's either ignoring me or he's not close enough to hear.

His footsteps get louder as he comes back up the stairs and passes me, his hands on my shoulders as he gently moves me aside and then flips a switch.

The front yard lights up. "Oh, my God, what the hell are you doing?"

"Quiet," he says. "I want you absolutely quiet until you can't stop yourself from screaming my name."

"That's never gonna happen."

"So you say now. And don't worry, I might want to fuck in public, but the whole point is to never let anyone see you but me. The lights are on the flower bed, not the porch."

He's right, I realize. I'm not lit up, I'm in the shadows. In fact there's just enough light to—"Hey." I squint my eyes at the dark shadow of his body as he walks down towards the street. "Where are you going?" I call. What the fuck? I want to take this blindfold off and see what the hell he's up to, but I don't want to spoil the game just yet.

A few seconds later his shadow jogs back towards me.

"Where did you go?"

"I was checking something across the street." He closes the front door to the house and pushes me up against it.

"A tripod, Shannon. I put a camera across the street zooming in on you."

Fuck.

There's plenty of cars going by on Broadway, so if anyone was looking real hard, they could probably see me. But it's late, so not many people.

He places something cold and hard in my hand. "Take it," he says.

It's a vibrator. The one we use to play. He loves to watch me masturbate. Especially when I'm in my bedroom at home. And even though he doesn't watch every night, I put on a show for him anyway. I'm like a fucking nympho these days. And when he doesn't fuck me, I'm desperate for an orgasm when I get home. Every once in a while he texts me a picture that he took while he was watching.

It makes me wet. Right now. It makes me wet just thinking about what he's doing.

"Get off," he whispers in my ear. "Right here, on my porch. With the screen door open and the camera rolling. I'm going to sit on the chair off to the side and do the same. And then I'm going to take you inside, play it back on the bedroom TV, and make you come again."

I take a deep, deep breath.

"Begin."

I press the controls on the vibrator until it's at full power, and then I place it between my legs, pressing it into my folds and letting out a sigh. All I hear are the cars and Mateo's breath hitching up a notch, but the thumping in my own chest soon drowns out those sounds.

"I like that," he says. "You should see yourself." And then he chuckles in that throaty way that drives me wild. "You *will* see yourself."

"What are you doing?" I ask, hearing his clothes rustle around.

"Taking my dick out and wrapping my fist around it."

"Tell me more, since I can't see you." This request gives me a little thrill. I've never had this much control over him before. I never get to ask him these things.

"The light is filtering in from the front yard so that it climbs up your body in a soft haze. I can see your pussy as you play with it." He scoots his chair across the concrete and the next time he talks, he's closer to me. "It's wet, isn't it?"

I press the vibrator against my clit, moving it around the way I like it. "It's ready for you, Mateo," I say. "Not this stupid piece of plastic."

"Yeah?"

I nod, biting my lip a little. "How much can people see?"

"When you watch the film you'll know. Now keep focused because I'm not letting you go inside until you come."

"Talk dirty to me. I need your help."

He chuckles. "I will, but not because you need my help. I've watched you dozens of times in your bedroom. What do you think about when you play with yourself, Shannon?"

"You, of course."

"My hard cock in your mouth."

I lick my lips. "Always. I want it now."

He moans and I can hear the friction he's creating with his pumping. "When I stand outside your window and watch you with your vibrator, I jerk off every time."

I start moving the vibrator faster, the sensations increasing. It's not cold out at night now that it's spring, but my nipples are bunched up in tight knots. "Why not just come inside and fuck me then? You know I'd never say no."

"I love that about you," he says, his breathing even heavier now. I hear more rustling and I can feel his body heat as he gets closer to me. His cock bumps up against my stomach, his fist vigorously moving back and forth, thrusting against my skin with each stroke. "I love that you never say no. But I like to watch you alone. You never give in completely when we're together. Always so guarded, even when you're naked. Always so careful, even when you're vulnerable. But in your own room, you let all that go and just relax. Do you feel safe there?"

"No." I laugh. "I feel safe with you."

He kisses my neck, one hand grasping at my hair, the other still working on his cock. "Right answer. You're always safe with me. Do you want to trade places?"

"And you put the blindfold on?" I ask.

He laughs and it rings out in the empty night.

"Shhh," I say.

"No, I'm not putting the blindfold on. I mean, do you want me to get you off and you get me off?"

I reach for his cock. He's so hard and the pool of wetness between my legs increases when he slips his finger inside me. "Oh," I moan softly. "I like that."

"You like when I stick things inside you, Shannon?" He takes the vibrator from my hand and pushes it into my pussy. I can only moan. "You like when I fuck you?" His fingertips roll my nipple and then pinch, making me gasp. But at the same time, he thrusts the vibrator in farther.

"Someone's walking down the sidewalk towards us, Shannon. If you don't come soon, he's going to turn his head when I make you scream. He's going to catch us. Probably stop and watch us. Do you want that?"

I think he's lying to make me nervous. It's working, but I still think he's lying. "No," I say, moving my hips to the motion of his hand with the vibrator. "No. I want to get off right now so you can take me inside."

"I think," he says, turning me around and taking each of my hands and placing them palms flat against the door, "I'd like to be fucking you from behind when that guy walks by."

"How far away is he?" I really can't tell if he's lying.

"Mmmm." Mateo thinks. "Maybe two minutes." And then he thrusts his dick inside me so hard, I gasp. "I like it loud. The louder you are, the faster I'll go."

"Mateo—"

He thrusts against my ass, his balls smacking my pussy. "Louder," he says. "Your turn to talk dirty to me."

OK, if there really is a guy coming, I need to be inside when that happens. And if there isn't, I still want to be inside. So I play along. "Reach around and play with my pussy. Rub my clit, Mateo. Rub it and make me come, and I'll scream your name loud enough to wake up the whole neighborhood."

He starts fucking me harder. He grabs my hip with one hand and snakes the other around my belly, fingers flicking back and forth across my most sensitive spot. I can feel my excitement building, but then he stops, reaches down for something, and brings the vibrator back up between my legs. He rubs it against my clit so hard, I begin to lose control. But when his finger unexpectedly slips inside my ass, I'm there.

He pounds me hard, the sound of skin against skin echoing through the night. I picture the man walking by, stopping to watch us. Mateo won't even know, his back is turned.

The vibrator thrums against me in just the right way, and I do exactly what he wanted.

I scream his fucking name.

He starts laughing, and then reaches over and turns the door handle so that we go tumbling into the small foyer.

"What the hell?" I ask, giggling on the floor next to him.

"Nice show," a voice calls from near the street.

"Fuck you," Mateo calls back. "You wish you saw something, asshole."

I rip the blindfold off and stare at him. "He did not see anything."

Mateo laughs and shrugs. "Nothing but my ass pounding you from behind."

We get up and take the party inside after that. He retrieves the camera and we watch the show from the point of view of the apartments across the street, laughing our asses off. Rolling around in bed, talking and being happy.

God, he makes me happy. Please, make him stay with me so I can stay happy.

"Last day of school," Danny says, walking up to me as I make my way to my locker in the back of the campus. "You ready?"

"So fucking ready," I say, smiling. I haven't seen much of Danny since he helped me with my ear. I see him at lunch and stuff. And he's been by talking to Jason a few times. Which is weird, but Jason was probably buying pot. I haven't smoked it since the semester started. Mateo is not into drugs. We really don't even drink all that much, unless we're having dinner at Alesci's and he sneaks me some wine with our food. But I am a new convert to the straight and narrow, so I have no room to criticize Jason in that department.

I do criticize him for losing interest in his daughter though. Kids are hard, and Olivia's easy infancy did him no favors in that department. He's drunk more, for one. And that's saying something since he's been getting drunk at least once a week since Jill died.

And I do hate the fact that he's almost never home. He's gone all day and then only home long enough to drop off Olivia before he goes to work at night. And there are lots of mornings when I wake up and his bed was not slept in and Olivia is just gone. She isn't as content now that she's six months old. She has a lot more opinions and Jason can't just give her a bottle and expect her to be satisfied.

She needs a lot of attention. And she's very loud when she doesn't get what she needs.

"So," Danny says. "What are your big post-grad plans? Marriage and kids with the man of your dreams?"

He's close. I do fantasize about that. But Mateo is leaving in two days for Arizona to help install the new software at the Phoenix Planetarium. That was his first sale post-Hawaii trip and since then he's set up a full year's worth of consultations around the country. He says he's even got international orders now. He officially became Dr. Mateo Alesci, PhD, last week after his defense.

It scares the fuck out of me, if I'm being honest. We're in totally different places. I can't go with him, obviously. I can't leave Olivia, especially when Jason has been acting so strange.

"Shannon?"

"Huh?"

"Big future plans?"

"Oh, well, I've been designing the websites for Alesci's restaurants. And Gigi wants me to make menus and marketing stuff next. So I guess I'm a graphic designer."

"Living the dream, huh?"

"Right."

"Why are you so pissy with me?"

"I'm not," I say, feeling very pissy right now.

"Please." Danny laughs. "I know you better than that. Trouble in paradise?"

"He's just working late tonight in LA, that's all. And he's leaving for Phoenix on Friday, so I'm feeling needy, I guess."

"Hmmm, working late in LA, huh?" Danny says. "I saw him a little while ago, so he must not've left yet."

"Where?" I ask, startled out of my funk. "He left last night."

"No, I swear. I saw him getting gas over by Vons."

I don't say anything to that, but inside I'm trying to figure out why Mateo would lie about going to LA last night.

"You should come to my party tonight and be needy with me."

"I don't think so. I have to watch Olivia, anyway."

"Nah, I heard Jason say he was leaving her at Dana's tonight so he can work. They're tight now, I guess. I never thought they'd make a good couple, but—"

"Dana? Wait. What?" I have to stop and shake my head. "Jason and the babysitter?" What the fuck is happening to this day? First Mateo and now Jason.

"You didn't know?" Danny looks at me like I'm an idiot. "How does that happen? He's been over there every day for months."

"He drops her off and goes to work all day."

"Is that what he told you?" Danny laughs. "Jesus Christ. Forget I mentioned it."

"Wait," I say, grabbing his arm so he can't walk off. "Tell me, Danny. He's fucking the babysitter?"

"Do you care?"

"Well, not really. But I do care that he's been lying to me all semester. I've been staying with Olivia every night almost so he can work that second job. Is he even working at night?"

"Oh, he's working. He's working for Phil, that's where he's working at. And that's the only job he's got as far as I know."

"Phil?"

"Dealing, Shannon. Like me, only he does the risky stuff. Runs to Tijuana and shit to pick up coke. That's why he's gone all night sometimes."

I almost fall over. "He's a drug runner for Phil?"

"How do you manage to stay so clueless?" Danny is looking at me like I'm a moron now. And I am. How didn't I know this? *Mateo*, that little part of my brain that makes sense says. Mateo is the only thing that's been on my mind.

"Didn't Mateo mention it?"

"Why would Mateo know about Jason?"

Danny has to blink several times at my apparent ignorance. "Are you fucking with me right now?"

"I mean, I know they know each other from high school and stuff."

"Did Mateo tell you that?"

"No, we never talk about Jason. Not really. Mateo asks about him casually, like if Jason's going to work at night and stuff, so Mateo knows he can bring me dinner."

Danny just stares at me. And then he laughs. And laughs, and laughs, and laughs.

"What?" I demand. "What's so funny?"

"Your boyfriend's a very talented liar, Shannon. I wanted to say something earlier, but it's none of my business, right? And you'd just assume I was making a move on you and then hate me afterward. But wow, I thought you had more street cred than this. The guy is a fucking narc. He's busted at least three major dealers in the past year alone. He works for the fucking Anaheim Task Force as an informant."

"How the hell do you know this? I mean, it's not like narcs go around announcing it."

Danny huffs out a long breath of air. "Oh, we all know it. He's had a long history. What the fuck do you think happened to my mom?"

"Your mom? What?"

"He busted her, Shannon. Right after high school. He was fucking her for drugs and then one day he decided to quit and go to college, and when she said she wasn't interested in his straight-edge lifestyle and dumped him, he turned her in. And do you know what he told me, Shannon? Do you know what he had the nerve to tell me as they were handcuffing my mom and taking her off to jail?"

I swallow hard and shake my head.

"He said, 'Hey, kid, it's for your own good.' I was eight years old, Shannon. Eight fucking years old. And I don't care how bad your fucking mother is, when you're eight years old, you love her no matter what."

"That really sucks, Danny. But Mateo is an astronomer now. He's been working on his PhD all semester. I saw his dissertation defense last week. That's what he does. He's not a fucking narc."

"Whatever," Danny says. "I don't know for sure that he's behind all those busts, but he's got a history of it. And I might not have a PhD, but I'm not stupid. I know how to draw a conclusion."

I don't know what to say. I walk over to the steps of a nearby building and take a seat before I pass out.

Danny comes and sits down next to me "Sorry, OK? I didn't want to be the one to tell you all this. I just figured you were smart enough to see through him. He's a liar, Shannon. A very gifted liar. And fucking weird, don't you think?"

Every moment we've had together runs through my mind. Weird. He could be. But I signed up for all of it too, so what does that say about me?

"He's gone tonight, right?"

I nod.

"Well, come over then. Just be a normal kid for once. I'm having a party to celebrate and I consider you a good friend. You should be there. We're graduating, Shannon. You worked your ass off this semester to make it happen. Let go for once and forget what that weird fuck has to say about it. I mean, really. Do you think he's gonna stick around now that he's finished with school? Come over and have fun with me. And I'm not making a move on you, OK? I've got my eye on someone and we've been fucking around for a few weeks. That's not what I'm after."

I sit and think for a few seconds. Maybe he's right. I'm way too dependent on Mateo for things. So I look up at Danny and say, "OK."

"Yeah?" He smiles.

"Sure. I need a good high-school party, to be honest."

"Come by around nine then." He stands up, smiling with his accomplishment of breaking down my walls. "Things will be just getting started by then."

He walks off, saying hi to other kids as he makes his way across campus. I just sit there and watch him disappear, thinking about what an idiot I am.

Jason, for one. That's probably all true. He's been lying to me.

But so has Mateo, at least a little, even if it's simply by not explaining. He never mentioned this history with Danny's family. But no wonder he wanted me to stay away from Danny. He can't be a narc, though. He's way too busy for that kind of secret life.

He has a secret life with me though. And I have one with him. And Jason has one with Phil and the babysitter. So it appears that it's not so hard to have a secret life.

I guess anything is possible. But I'm not throwing away anything with Mateo over his past with Danny's family. I love him way too much to do that.

I wish I didn't. Because Danny's right about one thing. Mateo is leaving Anaheim in two days and I'm not.

When I get home Danny was right. There's a note on the table in Jason's scratchy handwriting saying that Olivia is staying at the sitter's.

Why, though? Why tonight when he's never done this before? It just bugs me. And the whole secret relationship with the babysitter. Why is it a secret?

I sit down on the couch, not used to the quiet and freedom to be here and not have Olivia's demands be the first thing on my mind. I turn the TV on to make background noise, and still, I'm unsettled.

I don't think Mateo is cheating or anything stupid like that. But I just got a lot of information I didn't necessarily want. It's no big deal if he decided to go to LA today. Or if he got back early and didn't let me know. We don't have one of those report-back-to-me relationships. We hardly ever talk when we don't have plans. But we've had plans every day but Sunday for the past four months, so I never had to worry about where he was.

I get out my phone and press his contact button. It rings three times before he picks up, but the relief I feel washes over me like an ocean. "Hey," he says. "What's up? Have a good last day?"

"Yeah," I lie. I'm just happy to hear him. "What are you doing?"

"Just work," he says casually. "Cleaning out my office and turning things in."

"So you're still in LA?"

"Yup. I'm gonna stay here tonight. Got a hotel down the road."

"Oh, that sucks. I miss you."

"I miss you too," he growls. "But I'll make it up to you tomorrow. You have plans tonight?"

The first part of that response started out normal. But there's something in the last part that sets me on edge. "Why would I have plans?" I ask. "I have Olivia."

"You do," he says, after a few moments of hesitation. "Yeah, good then. Just forgot." There's a bunch of voices and then it becomes muffled, like he's covering the phone.

"Who's that?" I ask.

"No one. I gotta go, OK? I'll see you tomorrow."

"OK—" And then the call drops. I just look at the phone. "What the fuck was that?" But then my phone buzzes with an incoming text.

Mateo: Sorry, got cut off. I'm really busy, but I'll text you tonight when I finish up.

Shannon: You should come home tonight.

Mateo: Probably can't, but we'll talk later.

I don't text back, and he doesn't either. How did things get weird all of a sudden?

Maybe things have always been weird, Shannon? Maybe you just never noticed it before?

I sigh and throw my phone down on the cushion, bored out of my mind. For the first time this whole semester I have nothing to do and nowhere to be. No one is counting on me, and even though I resented the fact that I was taking care of Olivia all the time, now that she's not here I just want her back. Bad.

I swallow my pride and call Jason, just to check and make sure everything is OK. He picks up on the first ring.

"Yeah," he barks. I can hear Olivia crying in the background.

"Jason? Is Olivia OK? I got your note."

"Fine," he says absently. "Just hungry. I'm about to feed her now."

"I can watch her tonight, you know. She can stay here at home if you're busy."

"Nah, I'm gonna keep her with me. And I didn't want to have this talk on the phone, but since I've got you, you know that you can't stay anymore, right?"

"What?"

"I didn't want to tell you like this, but I've got a girlfriend. She has kids too. And our lease is up on Monday, Shannon. I'm moving away."

"Where?"

"Back to San Diego. I've got a restaurant job down there again. I'm taking this girl and her kids with me. She's gonna take care of Olivia from now on."

"Oh."

"You've got all weekend to find a place though. So you can stay until Monday. I already moved our shit out."

My throat starts to close up. "OK."

"Great, see ya around."

That call drops too and I just stare at the phone. I think my whole life just fell apart. My heart starts beating fast and I can feel the tears coming. It's not like I'm going to miss Jason, but just the thought of not being in Olivia's life breaks my heart. And he's replacing me with the babysitter, I just know it. I know she has two kids. He's probably been waiting for me to graduate all semester so they could move and leave me behind.

I look around and notice little things are missing. We didn't have much, but the small things that said *we live here* are gone. The apartment was furnished, except for the bedrooms, but when I walk down the hallway and into Jason's room, it's cleaned out. No bed, no crib, no diapers or bottles lying around. Everything is just gone.

I walk back to my room and flip on the lights. I have my futon and two cardboard boxes on either side of it that I use as nightstands. I have a few clothes in the closet, but that's it. I'm eighteen, I have no living relatives aside from a six-month-old baby, and my entire self-worth is contained in this bedroom.

I have a bank account and some money. Gigi has paid me every two weeks for the work I've put into the website. But it's not much. I get a little of that large payout with each check. Not enough to pay for an apartment in Orange County, that's for sure. I wondered all semester how Jason could afford this place. It might not look like much, but this is Colonial Anaheim and the rent is eighteen hundred a month. I guess that mystery is solved, since he's a drug runner for Phil and not an actual chef.

I could go back to Ohio. I could. It's a lot cheaper to live there.

But Olivia… I promised I would not leave her behind and now she's being taken away. Why didn't I see this coming? I knew Mateo was leaving, but Jason? It never entered my mind that he'd throw me away. I always figured he sorta needed me.

But he doesn't. He has the babysitter to fill my shoes.

I drop to my knees on the bed and then crawl to the pillows and start to cry. It's not a sobbing cry. I'm not that kind of girl. It's a silent one. The kind where the tears just fall out. I know I should be worried about where I will live next week, but all I see is Olivia's face. All I think about is her growing bigger, and learning to crawl, and talk, and walk. And I won't get to be there for any of it.

I have never felt this sad in my whole life. Not when my mother died. I had Jill then. We had a house and a car and I had all my friends and their parents coming by to make sure we were OK. I had teachers and neighbors who cared.

Not when Jill died. I was too scared of the future to mourn her properly. Too worried about Jason's erratic moods and Olivia's infant demands to take in how much I just lost with her death.

But this… I cry a little harder. Maybe I am that kind of cryer? This is so much worse. Because I have no one but Mateo. And he will leave me behind in two days when he goes out into the world to sell his software and make his dreams come true.

Do I even have dreams? No. I don't. I have thought about nothing but finishing school for months. And yeah, I have this little beginning of a career in web design. But my whole life has been wrapped up in sex and math. A baby and a bad brother-in-law.

I can think of no good way out of this, so I just fall asleep with tears on my pillow and an aching hole in my heart.

My phone is ringing out in the living room. I sit up, disoriented in the dark, then get up and find it on the couch where I left it earlier. "Hello?" I croak out, my voice still heavy with sleep.

There's loud music on the other end. "Shannon?" It's Danny. "You coming tonight?"

"What time is it? I fell asleep."

"What's wrong?"

How does he always know? "Nothing," I say. "I was just so tired, I fell asleep."

He says something else, but the music is so loud, I can't hear. And then the call drops.

I almost laugh at that. But what do I expect? When things start unraveling in my life, they don't stop until there's nothing left. I plop down on the couch and stare at the TV in the dark as all the things that happened today come rushing back.

A few minutes later there's a knock at the door. It opens without me even getting up. Danny Alexander stands in my doorway. "Shannon?"

He's backlit by the outside lights so all I see is a shadow. "What are you doing here?" I say from the couch.

He comes in, closes the door, and walks over to stand in front of me. "Why are you sitting in the dark?"

"Did you know Jason was moving to San Diego with that girl?"

"Um." Danny sits down next to me and frowns. He did.

"God, I'm so stupid."

"Jason's been around Phil's a lot lately. For work and stuff."

"I can't believe you call what he's doing work. He's a drug runner, Danny. And he's taking Olivia to San Diego. Did he ever have a restaurant job? Or has he always been doing these bigruns from Mexico?"

"Shit, Shannon, I'm not supposed to be telling you any of this. Phil would kick my ass, especially since you're dating Alesci."

"He's not a fucking narc, Danny."

"Whatever. But yeah, I knew. I figured you did too, Shannon. I had no idea Jason was skipping out on you."

"God, I really feel stupid."

"He's an asshole anyway. You're better off without him."

"I know that, Danny. But he's taking Olivia. And I know you don't know my whole story, but she's the last thing I have in this world. She's the only family I have, OK? And I need her."

He stars at me for a few seconds. "You don't know my story either. My mom never recovered from that bust. She got worse. She came out of jail so much worse than she went in. She was dealing drugs, doing drugs—"

"Then why do *you* do it?"

"I gotta make money to get the fuck out of here somehow. Might as well be the family business, right?" He laughs, but I don't. "Look, I don't deal like Phil or Jason. I sell joints. Pot is practically legal now. It's not the same."

"It will be the same if you keep doing it."

"I'm not going to keep doing it. I'm retired now. I sold the last of my stock a few days ago. No more high school, right? No more kids who want to get stoned at lunch or after school. Rocky and I are going to Santa Barbara for school at the end of the summer. Why do you think I was in the counseling office that day we met? Rocky and I had just gotten back from visiting the campus for recruitment week and my counselor wanted to know how it went. That's why you never saw me at Phil's over Christmas break."

How did I not know this about him? Why did I just assume he was a loser like me? "Great, so everyone is leaving this shithole but me. And I don't even belong here. Jesus Christ, can my life get any more fucking ironic?"

"I'm sorry," he says. "I didn't realize you were so attached to the baby. If I had, I would've..."

But he stops mid-sentence and drops that thought. "Would've what?" I ask.

He smiles. "I would've made more of an effort, you know? To fill you in on what's been going on."

"It's not your fault. I've just been so busy with my own life, I wasn't paying attention. I just wanted to assume Jason was a good guy."

"He's not," Danny says, looking down at me through the dark hair covering his eyes. "He's not a good guy, Shannon. And he should not be allowed to take that baby away."

"I agree. But I have no recourse. I'm her aunt. If he marries that girl, she'll probably have more right to Olivia than I do."

He sighs and then sinks back into the couch cushions next to me. We sit like that, thinking about the conversation for a few minutes. And then he says, "Let's go to the party."

I say nothing.

"Come on," he says, standing up and taking my hand, pulling me to my feet. "Let's think about this tomorrow. You know I'll help you any way I can, right?"

"I know." He will too. Say what you will about his uncle, and selling joints is really not a good way to pay your way through college, but Danny Alexander is a stand-up guy.

As we walk up the alley the music from his party gets louder and louder, and when we get to West Street, I can see that most of the fenced backyard is filled with people.

"Let's go in the front, I need to show you something."

"Sure," I say, feeling a little uneasy about the party. I'd rather be inside anyway. I'm not used to this anymore. I've been out of this scene for too long. And I have no real friends at Anaheim except Danny. There's no way Josie and Mary are at a party like this.

There are people on the front porch when we climb the stairs, and Danny stops to tell them all to go in the back. They grumble, but they finally go.

Danny sticks his key in the door and then stops, looking intently at me. "Don't be pissed, OK? I didn't know."

"Didn't know what?"

He just takes in a deep breath and opens the door. There's kids passed out on the floor. One about two, wearing nothing but an overfilled diaper. One is a little bit older and she's got on a dirty sundress. And there, on the other side of the girl in the dress, lying on a blanket, the only thing between her and the filthy hardwood floors, is Olivia.

"What the fuck?" I whirl around and see Dana, the babysitter, sitting on the couch, smoking and talking on her phone.

She looks at me, takes a second to recognize what's happening, and then she says, "Shannon's here."

"What the fuck?" I say again. "What the fuck is my niece doing at a drug house?"

I look at Danny and he tries a shrug. "I thought you knew," he says. "I swear to God, I thought you knew. She's been here for a couple months. Ever since Dana got evicted."

"What?" I look at Dana. "You live here? Since when? You lived down the street the last time I saw you."

"Well, I was supposed to live with Jason, but he said we had to kick you out first."

I run over and pick up Olivia, who is miraculously sleeping. "Is she even OK?" I ask Dana, feeling rage bubble up inside me as I check my poor little niece. "How the fuck is she sleeping with this party going on? Olivia?" I say, pressing my lips to her head. "Olivia?"

"She's fine," Dana says. And then I hear Jason's voice on the other end of the phone. "Here," she says, thrusting the phone at me. "He wants to talk to you."

I take the phone and spit, "You better have a good fucking explanation for this." Which is stupid. There is no good explanation for this.

"Just shut the fuck up, Shannon. She's not your concern anymore. And if you take her—" There's a scream of police sirens in the background and Jason says, "Fuck." And then the call drops.

"What the—" I look at Danny. "They're on a drug run?"

"You told her?" Dana screams.

"Yeah," Danny says, but he's talking to me.

"Well, I think they just got busted. There was a siren and then the call went dead."

"You bitch," Dana says, getting up from the couch and coming at me. Danny throws her off to the side. She crashes back into the cushions like a rag doll. She must be wasted.

"You let her take my niece while she's on drugs?" I ask Danny.

"Shannon—"

"Don't fucking Shannon me. In what world did you think I was OK with this?" He says nothing. "I'm so fucking out of here." I walk to the door and pull it open, but the cops are just pulling up, flashing their red and blue lights. "Jesus Christ."

Danny slams the door and points to the kitchen. "Let's go out this way. We can cut through the back." He grabs my arm and drags me down the hall. All the while Dana is screaming at us, still trying to get up from the couch where she fell.

He throws the door open and drags me down the back steps. The party is raging now. There are kegs and music is thumping so loud, no one even notices the police cars in the front yet.

Danny weaves us through the crowd of drunk and dancing people, and then Rocky yells for him just as the music stops.

"Fuck," he says, standing on his tiptoes, trying to see over a tall guy in front of us. The call comes again, and he whirls around, looking back at Phil's house. "Keep going," he tells me. "On the left side of the garage is a gate that leads out to the next street. Meet me there."

I look at the crowd of people I have to get through. "Shit, Danny." But when I look back, he's gone. I swallow hard, holding Olivia tightly to my chest. She's still asleep, even with all this noise. Something is definitely wrong with her.

I start pushing people out of my way and end up crashing into a short girl about my height. She spins around, beer spilling out of her red cup, and I say, "Sorry."

It's that girl I insulted back on the first day of the semester in front of the PE field.

"Oh, look who it is," she says, slurring her words. "*Pinche puta*. You're not fucking Mexican, huh? Then why do you live in my hood, bitch?"

I push past her, my eye on the prize. The back gate. But she grabs my arm, and when I turn around, there's a lot more of them now.

"Put the baby down, bitch," one girl says. She's a lot taller than me. And a lot meaner-looking too. "Or we'll kick your ass while you hold it."

"It?" I see red. "Touch me, and I'll cut your tits off and feed them to my dog, cunt. But if you do decide to mess with me, you better take your best shot, and you better make it good. Because you won't get a second chance." I am fluent in street venom. I can spew threats with the best of them. It works in my favor, because it stops the whole group of them for a moment.

And that moment is all I need, because someone yells, "Cops!"

Everyone starts screaming, and the girls turn. I bolt to the back of the property, slip alongside of the garage where Danny told me to go. And find a six foot tall chain-link gate.

Locked.

I turn around, panicked, and find the girls have followed me.

"Looks like a good spot to kick some ass," one says.

"I bet it'll take those pigs five minutes at least to make their way back here."

"That's more time than we need."

I let out a long breath and resign myself to a fight. I don't fight much. I'm not even that good at it. I depend on my mouth to talk my way out of things ninety-nine percent of the time. But these girls are not fucking around. They are gonna kick my ass. They come at me and the first one takes a swing at my face, but I duck, clutching Olivia to my chest.

Then the gate rattles and I whirl around and see Danny there with the key. "Get the fuck off, Maria," he snaps. "Get the fuck off her, or I swear, I will beat your ass myself." He opens the gate and lets me through as the girls try to follow, calling out insults. But Danny closes it back up and clamps the padlock together.

They scream at him. But he takes my hand and we run towards my street.

A car cuts us off and two officers get out with their guns drawn. "Down on the ground, Alexander!" they yell.

Holy fuck, I might have a heart attack.

Danny puts his hands up and looks at me. "I'm fine, don't worry. Whatever they're here for, it's not me." He kneels and then they come and push him face first into the grass, stepping on his back as they cuff him with those plastic zip tie things.

"Shannon!"

I spin around again and find Mateo climbing over the back gate where we just came out of.

"LA, huh?" Danny says up to me, still under the shoe of one of the officers.

I just stare down at him. And feel very, very sad. He was right. Why else is Mateo here?

34

"Are you OK?" Mateo asks. "What the fuck are you doing here?"

I just stare at him. And then Olivia stirs in my arms and I remember. "Oh, my God. I think something's wrong with my niece." I say it to the cops, not Mateo. Not Danny. I really need help and these guys are not the knights I imagined them to be. "She's not waking up right."

"Did you give her anything?" one cop asks.

"No," I say, shaking my head. "She was in there." I nod to Phil's house. "My brother-in-law left her with his girlfriend and I was taking her home. But something's wrong. I think she needs a doctor."

"I'll take them," Mateo says.

And if I didn't know it already, this is the clincher. Because one says, "OK, we got what we needed and all that's left is to search the house, but we're going to need to question her. So as soon as you take care of the kid, bring the girl down for a statement."

Mateo grabs me by the arm and starts leading me across the street. One of his cars is parked there—not the Camaro or the Mustang, one we've never driven in before. I've seen it in the garage.

I don't have a seat for Olivia and this makes me nervous, but her slow breathing and lack of response pushes that minor panic right out of my head.

259

I want to question Mateo. Ask him about so many things. But I can't stop hugging Olivia. "Something is wrong with her, Mateo. Hurry."

Mateo sticks a flashing light on the top of his car and speeds to the hospital where he pulls into the emergency drop-off. "Something's wrong with her," I tell the receptionist at the check-in desk. "She's not waking up. She's not breathing right."

"Sit down," Mateo says, pointing to a chair. "I'll take care of it."

"No," I say, getting pissed off. "This is an emergency. She needs help."

The receptionist picks up the phone and speaks to a nurse who must work in the back, and then she puts the phone down and says, "Have a seat."

I take a deep breath. I remember how long it took me to be seen when I came here for my ear and there's no way I'm going to sit quietly for an hour. "I'm not having a seat. I'll stand here all fucking night if I have to. I'm not having a seat. Get someone now."

"Ma'am," another receptionist says. "You're not the only emergency here."

"Goddammit," Mateo says to me. To me! "Go sit down and I'll handle it."

I don't sit down, but I walk away and watch as Mateo flashes some kind of ID at the lady. She nods and then calls the nurse again. He walks over to me and says, "They're coming right now."

"You just didn't want me to see that, right?" I seethe. "You didn't want me to know that you work for the police, right?"

He just stares at me. "Later, Shannon. Not here. Not now."

A nurse calls my name and I hurry over to the door where she's waiting. "What's the problem?" she asks, ushering me into the triage area and waving me into a room.

"I don't know, but she's sleeping and she won't wake up."

The nurse takes Olivia out of my hands and lays her down on the exam table. Olivia's head rolls to the side and her arms and legs are slack and motionless. I'd think she was dead if I couldn't see her chest rising and falling. But it's very slow. Too slow. Even I know this.

The nurse lifts one of Olivia's eyelids and shines a light in Olivia's eye. Then she places a tiny device on Olivia's big toe. A machine struts beeping nearby and I watch the lights dance on the display.

"What did she take?"

"What?" I ask, looking back at the nurse.

"Drugs. What kind of drugs did she get into?"

"She didn't take any drugs." But my stomach sinks.

"If she knows," the nurse says, looking at Mateo now, "she needs to tell me. It will save a lot of time and maybe the baby's life."

"Shannon, what did you give her?"

"Me?" He did not just say that. "I didn't give her anything."

"It looks like opiate overdose. Pinpoint pupils, depressed respiration, and no response to stimuli."

"What?" Oh, my God. Jill's death is flashing back to me. "No," I say, shaking my head. "That's not possible. That can't happen."

She pushes a button and an alarm starts. "You're going to have to wait outside," she says, pushing me out of the room while people rush in with a crash cart. "Take her to the triage waiting area," she tells Mateo.

"Come on, Shannon," Mateo says, leading me by the arm again.

"Will she be OK?" I call. But no one answers me.

We end up down the hall and through a doorway, where there's a small waiting area with a few people looking just as distraught and worried as me. I sit down where Mateo places me, and then he gets a call, checks his phone, and leaves me sitting there.

What the hell is happening? Everything is wrong. Everything is bad.

I sit there in silence for a few minutes, trying to find something—anything—that will help me make sense of my life right now.

I can't come up with a single thing.

"Shannon?" Mateo says, sitting down in the chair next to me.

"I don't even want to talk to you right now."

He lets out a low laugh. "Well, you're gonna need to. I have a lot of questions."

"Me too," I say, looking up at him. "But I don't have time for you right now, Mateo. I can't hear any more lies."

"Lies?"

I huff out a long breath. "You busted Jason tonight? And Phil? Some drug bust, right? Those cops at Danny's house said you guys got what you needed. You wanna tell me what that was?"

"You can't possibly be sticking up for them. Tell I'm hearing you wrong." He stares at me like I'm a stranger.

"Did you bust them?"

"We did. They deserved it. You're better off, Shannon. It's for your own good."

"What?" I ask. "What did you just say?" Danny's remark about what Mateo said to him when they carted his mother off comes back to me.

"He was hitting you, right? Jason? And regardless of how highly you think of Danny Alexander, Phil Alexander is a whole other story. He was responsible for seven deaths back when we were friends, Shannon. Sold a shitload of coke cut with fentanyl. I bet Danny Alexander didn't tell you *that*, did he?"

"What?"

"Fucking figures. Just play stupid a little more, why don't you."

"I'm not playing stupid. I'm not from here, Mateo. I have no way of knowing the history of you people. And if that was something I should've *known*"—I seethe the word—"then you should've been the one to tell me. Not him."

"Well," Mateo says, sighing. "It's done now. Jason and Phil got caught moving sixty pounds of coke across the border. They're going away for a very long time."

I just look at my hands. "I'm happy about that. I am." I look up at Mateo. "I'm not sticking up for them. But I don't need you to decide what's good for me."

"You sure the fuck do. Because you've made a lot of stupid mistakes since we've met."

"Yeah," I say, looking him dead on. "And my biggest one was trusting you."

We sit in silence after that. I'm so done with him.

After about an hour two cops come through the waiting room doors. Mateo and I are the only ones left in here. I don't even know why he stayed. But he gets up and meets them at the door, and then they go back into the hallway to talk.

I cannot believe it's ending this way. Did he even like me? Or was he using me the whole time just to get to Phil and Jason? He was probably watching me at night to see if I was dealing too. And hey, if you've got to keep your eye on an eighteen-year-old girl, why not fuck her in the process?

I feel sick.

"Shannon?" Mateo says from the door. The two cops are next to him, but they walk towards me. One is holding something in his hand. "They need to ask you some questions. You need to be honest."

"I *am* honest," I growl at him.

"Miss Drake," the one officer says. "Do you recognize this bottle?"

I look at the thing the other officer is holding in his hand. I take it and read the label. "Yes. This is my codeine prescription from when my ear got infected."

"So it *is* yours?"

"Yes. It's got my name on it. It was a legit prescription. Why?" I have a very bad feeling about this.

"Miss Drake," the other cop says. "We're gonna read you your rights. You have the right to remain silent."

"What?" I look up at Mateo and he's frowning, but makes no move to explain.

"Anything you say can and will be used against you in a court of law."

The other cop takes me by the wrists and places me in handcuffs. "What did I do?" I look at Mateo, pleading. "Tell me what I did!"

"You have the right to an attorney. If you cannot afford an attorney, one will be provided for you. Do you understand the rights I have just read to you? With these rights in mind, do you wish to speak to me?"

"Yes, of course! I didn't do anything."

"Miss Drake, your niece is experiencing an overdose of codeine. We believe the pills came from this bottle. Did you feed your niece codeine to make her sleep?"

"No! Of course not! I would never do that! Mateo?" I look at him. "Tell them I'd never do that."

"I did, Shannon. But you told me on the phone tonight that you were taking care of her."

"I wasn't! She was with Jason's girlfriend. I took her out of that house. I found her like this!"

"She's going through withdrawals, Miss Drake," the cop who read me my rights says. "They've moved her to Children's Hospital for treatment. This has been going on for months. They think she was born addicted. Dana Alexander told us something of your sister's past an she admitted that Jason was lacing the baby's formula with codeine to make her sleep."

"Dana Alexander is the one who was taking care of her. And my brother-in-law was the one who always fed her! I didn't give my baby niece drugs to make her fall asleep!"

The cop with the handcuffs takes me by the arm and leads me towards the door. "It should be easy enough to prove, Miss Drake. Try not to get too upset. We're booking you in tonight, but Mateo said he'd bail you out, so it won't be long. You need to show up in court tomorrow."

I look at Mateo as I pass him and see nothing but disappointment.

He thinks I did this.

He really thinks I did this.

35

I am booked into the jail. They fingerprint me and take a fucking mug shot. That's what they do when they arrest you. I have a court appearance scheduled for nine AM, but Mateo insisted as they took me away that he'd have me out in a few hours.

Well, it's been more than a few hours.

And even though I want to scream and shout that I am getting blamed for something I didn't do, there is this little niggling thought in the back of my head that I deserve this.

I should've noticed something was wrong. Do babies really sleep that much? I wouldn't know, I've never had a baby. But there's this thing called the internet and I've had access to it for most of my life. One search was all it would've taken to look some of this up. One search after Jill died about the possibility of opiate addiction in babies was all it would've taken.

I could blame Mateo. I want to blame Mateo, if I'm honest. And there are so many ways I could justify that copout. But he's not her aunt. He wasn't living with her for the past six months.

I could blame Jason. He's the one who drugged his kid to make her sleep, so it really is his fault. Maybe that Dana chick participated, I wouldn't know. But I knew Jason was a bad guy from the start. I didn't need Danny Alexander to tell me that.

I look for Danny at the jail, since presumably he was booked in too. But there are only women in here. Some of them I recognize from the party. Even one of those gang girls who tried to fight me. She's not looking so tough now.

The place gets more and more busy as the morning approaches and then a guard comes and says, "Drake?"

I get up, but he waves me back. "Alesci said to hold tight." And then he walks off.

The gang girl snickers at me. "I guess the narc's girlfriend doesn't get off as easy as she thinks."

My spirits sink even deeper. As mad as I am at him, I had a little hope that he'd come through and get me out of here.

Welcome to eighteen, Shannon. The age when life gets to kick your ass over and over and all you get to do is stand there and take it. I didn't think anything could suck worse than seventeen, but obviously I am lacking the wisdom of experience, as Mateo pointed out when we first met. Because my adult life has been nothing but non-stop bullshit.

I sigh and lean my head back, watching the minutes tick by on the clock, and when morning finally comes and the place gets busy with the activities of a new day, they come for us and chain us together like prisoners.

I can only hang my head as they lead us out to the hallway and tell us to keep on the right side of a yellow line that divides it down the middle. I'm last, so I follow along until they stop us at the door and unchain us from each other as we enter another holding cell.

"Drake," a guard says, putting his hand up to prevent me from entering the cell. "You have a personal appearance in front of the judge. Stay here."

I stay. The prisoners are told how to behave and that they will be on closed-circuit TV for their appearance. Then he closes the door and uncuffs me. "You're going home, so relax."

"How do you know?"

"Alesci has been talking to Judge Otero for two hours. They're dropping the charges. But you still have to make an appearance."

The relief is real. It floods through my whole body and I suddenly want to cry.

"Just hold it together a little bit longer, OK?" the guard says in a sympathetic voice. "We know it wasn't you. There were other kids at that house last night and they tested positive for drugs too."

"Do you know how my niece is doing? She was taken to the hospital last night for an overdose." I sob the word. I can't believe my little niece had an overdose. "She's only six months old."

"I think she's OK. I think we would've heard if it had gone bad. We arrested Dana Alexander too. And we would've charged her with attempted murder instead of child endangerment if anything was happening at the hospital."

I bite my lip and try to stop crying.

"Come on. Alesci is waiting for you in court."

I am led down more hallways and the guard keeps his hand on my arm as we walk. We stop in front of a door and we are buzzed through. It leads directly into the courtroom and I see Mateo and another man at a table on the far side. They are both wearing suits.

Mateo smiles when he sees me, and I swear to God, I just want to go home and cry. But the courtroom is packed with people, and I am taken over to a table in front of Mateo and told to sit.

Mateo leans over the railing that separates us. "You OK?" he asks.

"I don't know," I tell him honestly as I turn in my chair to see his face. "Is Olivia OK?"

He nods. "She will be. We'll talk about that later. But right now, you just have to sit and let the lawyers do their thing, and then I can take you home."

I turn back around and face forward. I don't even *have* a home.

The judge enters and the bailiff asks us to rise. Then he tells us to sit and they start calling my case. "The People vs. Shannon Drake."

I want to die right now.

But then the lawyers start talking and in three minutes, the judge pronounces the charges dropped. Mateo shakes my lawyer's hand and then takes mine, leading me out of the courthouse.

I hang my head again. I never look up to see all those people as they gawk at us. We walk out to the parking lot in silence, in the chilly morning air, and then he holds my door open to his car.

I get in and lean my head against the window.

He sighs as he closes his door. "You OK?"

"I want to see Olivia."

"You can't."

I look at him. "What do you mean?"

"It was part of the deal. No contact with her until there's a complete investigation with Social Services. Weren't you listening in there?"

"I was too busy worrying about being charged with drugging her, so no, sorry. I missed the legal jargon about them taking my only family member away."

"Shannon," he says, using that voice I've come to associate with his sexual requests. It makes my stomach turn. "You were almost implicated in a child endangerment case. You had her at a known drug house last night."

"I was taking her home!"

"I get that," he growls. "But there's a procedure to these things."

"Fuck your procedures," I say. "I didn't do anything wrong. I don't ever do anything wrong, Mateo. So why the fuck do I always have to do penance for other people's mistakes?"

He starts up the car without commenting and we stay angry and silent as we make our way back to his house. I don't wait for him to get my door, just jump out and start walking down his driveway.

"Where the fuck are you going?"

"Home," I snap.

"You can't go home, Shannon. It's a crime scene. They got a warrant last night to search for drugs. It's taped off and you can't go in."

"Great." I throw up my hands. "Just fucking great." I want to scream so bad. I want to yell at the entire world right now.

"Just come inside."

I laugh. "You think we're still together?"

"Why wouldn't we be?" he sneers.

He's serious. He's actually fucking serious. "You lied to me."

"It was my job, Shannon."

"Was I your job? Did you get to know me so you could bust Jason and Phil?"

I wait for the answer I so desperately need to hear, but it never comes.

"Great, that's just great. You've been playing me all right. But not like an instrument."

"That's not true," he says, reaching for my hand.

But I shake it off. "Then what part's true? Did you know about Jason before we met?"

"Yeah." He nods.

"So it is true. You used me, Mateo."

"I didn't use you, Shannon. Everything we had was real."

"Except for the parts that weren't, right? How could I ever believe you? Especially after you told me all those lies when we first met."

"That was fantasy talk and you know it."

"How do I know it? It's a serious question. How the hell do I know which parts are true, which parts are lies, and which parts are fantasy? Did you really see me when I was walking to Bill's to get food?"

"Yeah."

But I can hear the 'but' he left unsaid. "But you already knew me, didn't you?"

"Shannon—"

"No." I stop him with a hand to his chest. "Leave me alone."

I turn and walk down his driveway and make a left at the street.

"Where are you going?" he calls. "Shannon!"

I ignore him, just keep walking until I get to the street I normally take to school and turn left again.

"Slow down, dammit. Where are you going?"

Mateo follows me, asking that question over and over. Asking me to stop and slow down over and over. But I just keep walking until I am standing on Lincoln Avenue in front of the school.

"What the fuck are you doing?"

I cross the street at the light and start heading towards the front steps.

"Shannon," Mateo growls as I start climbing them. "What the fuck are you doing?" He grabs my hand again, making me stop and whirl around.

"I'm gonna have a conversation with Mr. Bowman, Mr. Alesci. And I'm gonna tell him what I should've told him four months ago."

He just stares at me, his green eyes searching mine for answers. He's not panicked, and that surprises me. But he does look slightly nervous.

I turn back to the steps and continue climbing and then I open the front door. It's eerily silent since school ended yesterday. The lady I know is at the front reception and I make my way over to her. "Is Mr. Bowman in?" I ask.

"Oh, hi, Shannon." She eyes me warily. I must be a mess after spending the night in jail. "He's around here somewhere. Let me look."

She walks off and the door opens behind me. I glance over my shoulder and Mateo walks in, his face long and his expression sad. He walks up behind me and takes my hand. "I'm not gonna let you tell him."

"Like hell—"

"Stop," he orders with a finger to my lips. "I'm not going to let you tell him because I'm gonna tell him myself. I'm not walking away, no matter how mad you are or how hard you push. *I'm not leaving.*"

36

"Shannon?" Mr. Bowman says, coming up behind us. He takes one look at Mateo's hand in mine and then his face goes angry. "What's going on, Mr. Alesci?"

Mateo holds our hands up. "I love her, OK? We've been together the whole semester and I love her. I'm gonna marry her, Bowman. And she earned her grade, I swear to God, she earned her grade. She's a trig genius now, even if she did learn about triangles while she was naked—"

"Oh. My. God!" I say. "Stop talking, you dumbass! I was just gonna ask him for help with Olivia!"

"And I realize she's pissed off at me right now, and it doesn't look like I have a chance in hell in getting her to come home with me again, let alone marry me. But I'm a come-from-behind kind of guy, Mr. Bowman." He looks at me and grimaces. "And I don't mean to imply we're having anal sex, Shannon, so don't freak out on me." And then he turns back to Bowman. "But she loves me back. She told a whole auditorium filled with kids in Hawaii that she did, and I'm holding her to it. So there." He throws up his hands. "She's mine, goddammit, and I don't give a fuck what you say about it."

"You're done now?" Bowman asks. The ladies in the office start to giggle.

"Just kill me now," I mutter.

Mateo lets off a long breath. "No, actually. She's got something say, so no. We're not done. You can take it from here, Shannon."

I seriously want to die.

"Perhaps," Bowman says, glaring at the office ladies, "we should go somewhere private?"

Mateo sighs and takes my hand and we follow Bowman out of the office and down the hallway to an empty classroom. He walks to the front and Mateo and I sit in two student desks in front of the larger one where Bowman leans back, his arms folded over his chest.

He glares at Mateo. "I trusted you with her," he seethes. "I explained that she was very vulnerable. And what did you do? You took advantage of her."

Mateo sighs and looks over at me. "I'm sorry," he says. "I'm sorry if you think that, but I'm not sorry for what I did last night. Phil Alexander was dangerous. Jason, as you well know, Shannon, was dangerous. I got them off the streets. So I'll apologize for not giving you time to recover from the death of your sister, for being a shitty teacher, for being a liar, and for being…" He glances at Bowman real fast and then back to me. "For being… insistent that you were mine."

He looks at Bowman again. "But I will not apologize for loving her. I don't care what you say about it, what we have is good. The way I got her to trust me was the best I could do, and she passed that class by working hard. So if you think you're going to try to take that away and stop her from graduating, I'll fight you over it, Bowman. I will. She can retake all those tests and she will pass every single one."

They glare at each other for several moments and then Bowman looks over at me. "Is that how you feel, Shannon?"

"God." I sigh. "I'm really not here to discuss my love life, OK? It's none of your business anymore, Mr. Bowman. I don't need help with Mateo. You said I should come to you if I needed help with Olivia. Well, I need help. I really, *really* need your help." And then it all comes spilling out. I tell him everything I never wanted him, or anyone, to know about me. I tell him about Jill, about Jason, about the drugs, the violence. Everything.

And when I'm done I let out a deep breath. "So will you help me?"

He looks sad. With each new revelation about what's really been going on, his expression gets more and more concerned. But now he just looks sad. "I failed you. Completely failed you."

"You didn't," I insist. "I didn't tell anyone how bad it was. Not Danny, not Mateo, not you. I just want to know if you can help me get Olivia back."

"I have to be honest, Shannon. It's not looking good. My wife is a social worker and I know from experience that they do not let many younger relatives take care of infants. Especially those who failed to notice the signs of drugging over a long period of time. As you have found out the hard way, new adults don't have the experience to handle some things. Or the money, or the time, or the commitment."

"We're committed," Mateo says.

"We?" Bowman sneers. "So you're volunteering to take care of this child? You don't even know her."

"I know *her*," Mateo growls. "I might not know Olivia, but I know Shannon. And we're not going to stop until we get that baby back. With or without your help, Bowman. We're getting her back."

Maybe Mateo isn't such a bad guy.

But Bowman is looking like he's about to blow a gasket. "Look," I interrupt his explosion. "I'll do whatever it takes. I understand that I don't have much experience in being an adult. I know I'm only eighteen. But I'm smart. You said so yourself. And I've got a bright future. You said that too. So help me. I did everything you asked this semester, even though none of it was fair or even logical. I did the work once and I'm willing to do it again."

He looks at me, thinking.

"Please," Mateo says. "She needs that kid, Bowman. And that kid needs her. Don't let them take away the only thing Shannon has left."

Bowman takes his time as he sorts us out in his mind. "It's not going to be easy," he finally says.

"We don't care," Mateo replies. "We'll do whatever it takes."

"It's not going to be immediate, either. They are notoriously slow in Social Services."

"That's OK," I say. "I want them to do it right."

"It's going to require a lot of sacrifices."

"We're willing to make them," Mateo says, reaching for my hand across the aisle. He squeezes it, but his eyes never leave Bowman.

After several agonizing seconds, Bowman sighs. "I'll call my wife and see what I can do."

He leaves us after that, saying he will get in touch when he hears something, and Mateo and I get up out of the students' desks and look at each other.

We don't say anything. He just leads me out of the building, down the stairs, and we walk home in silence. When we get in front of his house he says, "You're coming in."

It's not a request.

I follow him into the house and sit at the kitchen table. "Thank you," I say, as he sits across from me. "I appreciate what you said back there."

"I meant every word, Shannon."

I nod.

"What?" he asks. "Why aren't you saying anything?"

I stare into his green eyes. He's fucking handsome. His body is hot, he's good in bed, he's smart, he's got money, and a bright future. He helped me this semester in so many ways. He helped me pass trig and he fed me. He took me on dates, to Hawaii, and he made me feel so good when we were together.

But...

"I don't think I know you." I expect him to laugh at that. Pass it off as silly. It might be silly. I know a lot about him. "I don't think I have the faintest idea of who you are. But more importantly, I don't know me either. I have no idea who I am right now. I have lost every identity I've scratched out for myself over the past eighteen years and I feel like I'm standing at day one."

He watches me as I try to figure things out.

"It's scary, Mateo."

"It doesn't have to be, Shannon."

But I nod my head. "It really does. I think while I was in here getting used to your overpowering nature I lost sight of that. And if I let you help me—"

"Shannon."

"If I let you be the reason I make it, the reason I get Olivia back, the reason why things turn out OK, then that's it, Mateo. I'm done. I will never, ever stand on my own again. You will bulldoze me through life."

"Shannon, please."

But I shake my head. "I don't even know what I want yet. I want Olivia, I like a lot of things you and I did together. But I'm not choosing you…"

I really do mean to say more. I really don't mean to make it sound the way it does. The way I leave it. But I stop talking right at that moment. I stop talking so his last impression is one of rejection.

I stand up and say, "You should go to Arizona tomorrow."

"Why are you doing this? To get even with me?"

I turn my back to him. "To get over you. I know you meant what you said back there at school, and I appreciate that. But you had your chance to be eighteen. You made your decisions." I look over my shoulder. "It's time for me to make mine. I don't want to be saved, Mateo. Regardless of what you think, I'm not looking for someone to tell me what's best, or keep me in check, or make life less scary. What is life without risk? And what is risk without fear?"

He has nothing to say to that. Mateo Alesci is struck speechless as I walk out of his house and cross Broadway. I make my way to my apartment and sure enough, there's that little yellow tape over the front door.

Fuck them. Jason's stuff is gone, it's just my stuff being held hostage. I'm just about to rip the tape off the door when a voice calls out behind me.

"Wanna come inside, Shannon?"

I turn around to see the cop chick across the quad, peeking her head through her screen door. She's got her blonde hair up in a ponytail and her uniform on.

"Are you going to bust me if I go inside and get my things?" I yell.

"No," she calls back. "No one really cares. I'm sure they got what they needed last night."

"Were you a part of it too? Is that why you moved in?"

"Maybe a little bit," she concedes. "But not the way you think. I knew what the task force was up to, but that's not why I asked you if you were OK that day."

"Then why?"

"Why?" She laughs. "Because I care." She opens her door wider and repeats her offer. "Want to come inside?"

"I really don't," I say back. "I just need to sleep. And I might not have much in there, but it's mine. And I need it right now."

"I get it. I do. And if you ever want to come talk, feel free. We can be friends." She smiles at me, then closes her door and disappears inside.

I don't want any more friends right now, so I open the front door to my apartment and go inside. It's not trashed like you see in movies. Of course, we really had nothing. And Jason took everything that was his and Olivia's when he left yesterday. My room has a few things out of place, but the bed is just fine.

I strip out of my clothes, take a shower, dress in shorts and a tank top, and spend the whole day curled up under a blanket in my dark room.

I do not sleep for one moment. My eyes close, but all I see are the mistakes I made.

Maybe this is why people kill themselves?

My whole life can be contained in a backpack. It makes me laugh. I have four days before I'm kicked out of this apartment, I have about—

A sharp knock on my window scares the shit out of me. Mateo stares back from the other side, and then he slides the window open and points his finger at me. "You know what?"

"What?" I growl. I'm so annoyed at him for interrupting my thoughts.

"Fuck you. Fuck you, Shannon. You don't get to fucking wallow in pity and call me a bulldozer."

"Get out."

"No. I'm not even in, so I'm not getting out. I'm sticking around. How about that? You're not gonna get rid of me that easy. And you know what else? I paid your fucking rent. Now what are you gonna do?"

"What?"

"I've lived in this neighborhood most of my life. You don't think I know who owns this building? So you can't just leave. You're paid up for six months."

"What the fuck are you doing?"

"I'm saving you, bitch."

I almost crack a smile.

"OK?" he says. "I'm fucking saving you whether you want it or not." He holds up a brown paper bag with a receipt stapled to it. "And I brought lasagna. So try to say no to that. I dare you."

"Mateo—"

"No, dammit. *No.* I'm good for you. I'm good. For. You. And I totally understand what you're saying. You need space, you need to make your own way. You need all the things I got when I was your age. But you can still do that and be my girlfriend. It's not a zero-sum game, Shannon. Life isn't all or nothing, it's something in between. So here," he says, holding the lasagna bag out. "I know you're hungry, so I brought you dinner. You don't have to come over, you don't have to let me in, hell, you don't even have to talk to me. But I'm still here. I'm always gonna be here." He balances the bag on the window sill. "I'll just be across the street."

And then he turns away and walks through my gate, slamming it behind him.

I sit there for a few moments, stunned. But then the smell of lasagna wafts in and my stomach grumbles so loud, and so forcefully, I get up grab the bag. When I do, I look out onto the patio and see a candle on the little table.

What the fuck?

I take the bag and go out into the living room, staring at the little flickering flame through the slider. What did he do now?

I walk through the door and smile.

It's set up like an Italian restaurant. Red-checked tablecloth, menu, silverware, plate, and next to the candle is a little mechanical pencil. I sit down, rip the receipt off the bag, and unfold it to reveal a full sheet of paper. Two actually. I hold it near the dim candlelight so I can read it.

It's a list of fucking trig problems. With a puzzle on the back side that I am supposed to solve. The second sheet is a blank piece of paper that says, *Show your work.*

"Jesus Christ," I say. But I say it with a smile.

I work the problems as I eat, and by the time I'm done, I have the message.

I like you, it says. *Keep going.*

He said that to me back when we first met. It was a way to let me know that what we were doing was real and I shouldn't be scared.

We're still real, is what his message really says.

I flip the second piece of paper over. I only used one side to solve the problems, so I make my own code for him to solve. My problems are stupid and easy. Two plus two and three times five kind of stuff. But the problems don't need to be hard for him to get the message.

I need more than the answer. I need the process.

When I'm done, I walk across the street and find him sitting on his porch, waiting for me. We don't say a word. I just open the screen door an inch, slip the paper between it and the doorjamb, and then walk back the way I came.

I can hear his chuckle just as I slip through the gate into the apartments that are not mine. And I smile all the way past the pool, out into the alley, back into my own patio, and through my sliding door.

The next morning when I wake up and look out on the patio, the table has been cleared of the Italian restaurant, and there sits another bag and a cup of coffee. I rip the receipt off and open it up.

Another problem. Much harder to solve than yesterday's.

I look inside the bag. Donuts.

I work as I eat and the message at the end is…

I'll be back on Tuesday.

He left for Arizona. I'm happy he left. We need to find ourselves right now. Find our places in this world. He worked hard for his PhD and he deserves to move forward. We both deserve to move forward because we passed a milestone in our lives, and now we're about to start something new.

37

I hold Olivia in my arms as we sit in the judge's chambers. She's so big now. And she's turning one next week. She looks so much like Jill with her blonde hair and blue eyes, I want to cry sometimes.

"So the test came back," I say, picking up our conversation. I've been coming to see this judge for almost six months. We meet once a week with Olivia in my arms just like this. "Jason's not the father."

"I see," Judge Otero says. "That was smart, Shannon. No one contested it until you thought to ask for paternity."

"Yeah, well, his parents weren't getting her. No way. They didn't do such a great job with him. What makes them think they'd do any better with her?"

Judge Otero smiles. "The past can certainly dictate the future. But not always."

"I just don't like them."

"Me either." He laughs.

"I'll be nineteen in a couple months. I think I can handle it now, Judge." Olivia does not live with me yet. I had to prove myself and she's been staying with foster parents. But I see her every day. I want to make sure she knows she belongs with me. "I have a good job designing websites. Have you seen the new Alesci's Anaheim delivery page?"

"I have," he says. "My wife and I used it last night. I'm impressed, Shannon. You've worked hard. You took parenting classes and CPR. You started your own business, got your license and bought a car."

"Mateo bought the car, Judge. I can't take credit for that." Mateo and I have not talked in person since the night he came to my window, but we've sent each other hundreds of messages via codes. If he's in town, we send messages twice a day sometimes.

Judge Otero smiles. "It's a nice car. I wish I had one just like it."

The car was the first present Mateo gave me and it's brand new. *Best safety features on the market*, was the message in that night's code.

"Have you talked to Danny?"

I nod. "Yeah, he stayed with me a couple of weekends ago when he came home from school for a visit. We went out and had dinner and stuff."

"No regrets there?"

"No." I laugh. We've had many, many long talks about Danny. He did go to jail the same night I did, but he was never charged either. "Just a friend. A very good friend."

"I like him. He's worked hard to change his life as well. And I'm glad he and his sister got away from that family."

"Me too," I agree. "You don't get to choose your family, right?"

"Right," Judge Otero says. "You're stuck with them until you're old enough to choose your own. He'll find a new one. He's on his way."

"I think I'm on my way too." I don't want to push Judge Otero into a decision. I understand that learning to be a responsible parent takes time. But I really want to move forward and I want today to be the day.

"Have you made a decision about where you'll live?"

My lease is up in a few days. Mateo paid for the first six months, and that's just about over. "I... I don't know yet. I might be seeing Mateo tonight?" It comes off as a question because it's not really up to me. "His last code said, *Congratulations*. So I think he's expecting a celebration. But..." I hesitate. "It's up to you. And I respect your decision, Judge. So if I'm not ready yet..." I have to stop because I want to cry. But I gather myself together and take a deep breath. "I'll accept that."

I'll go home and sob is what I'll do, but I'm not going to try to influence his decision with that threat. I'm done skating through life. I want to earn it. I need to work for it.

He looks down at my file and then signs a piece of paper. "I think you're more than ready, Shannon. I think you're going to make a great mother."

He leans forward and takes Olivia's little hand. She loves him to death and shoots him a smile. "You had a rough start for sure. But your mommy loves you a lot."

It was difficult weaning her off the codeine, but she's better now. She no longer cries because of the withdrawal, and the foster family did such a great job with her. I'm eternally grateful.

Judge Otero looks back at me and smiles. "Tell Mateo that congratulations are indeed in order and I wish you both the best."

My heart thumps like crazy when Shannon pulls into my driveway. We agreed months ago that she needed to do this herself. She needed to find her own solution to this problem. And that when she was ready, and things were in order, she'd come here and we'd talk in person again.

Maybe the codes were silly, but it was the only way she knew how to communicate with me. She wanted to start over and I didn't. I wanted to keep going. But even though she doesn't have the wisdom of experience, she's the smartest person I know. Because she was right.

We needed a new beginning. One where the power was shared and the secrets were over.

She gets Olivia out of her baby seat in the back of the car, and I can see Shannon wiping her tears from the kitchen window. But they're happy tears. Everything is good right now or she wouldn't be in my driveway.

I've stood here in this spot every Wednesday at six o'clock for months waiting for this moment. And each time she didn't come, I missed her more. I'd sit down and write her trig problems, trying to find the perfect message to make her feel better about not getting the thing she wanted most.

Her own family.

I wait at the window to see what she will do, and she walks to the back porch.

There are a few moments of hesitation. She chews her lip as she raises her hand to knock.

But she doesn't knock.

She reaches for the handle and opens the door, letting herself in. I hold my breath as I smile, unable to dare to believe it's finally time.

But then she speaks and everything is right in the world.

Because she says, "We're home."

End of Book Shit

Welcome to the End of book Shit, fondly called the EOBS around these parts. This is where I get to say anything I want about the book.

So let's get right to the point. Is this really a true story? Yes and no. Lots (and I do mean lots) of things in this book are 100% true, but it's a called a novel for a reason. It's based on my story when I was eighteen, but it's obviously been embellished.

The first thing I'd like to talk about is Anaheim High School. Yeah, lots of those things about it were true, that first chapter is 99.9% true. That really happened to me. I was x number many credits ahead, yet they told me I was not going to graduate unless I went to night school and made up math, science, PE, and driver's ed. Anaheim High School had its problems back when I was there in 87, and I'm sure it's got its problems today. But that counselor (who was not named Bowman) really did give a shit and really did help me get through it. Also, the girl I insulted never did try and beat me up. I did see her at a party later in the semester, but it was all good. I had no issues with the kids there at all. They were good kids.

The name Shannon comes from my best friend from childhood in Ohio. I saw her a few months ago and after discussing all the crazy shit we got into, told her I was gonna make her a character because we were WILD. Just fucking wild when we were teens. And she said do it. So thanks, Shan. Love ya, bitch. Hope you like the book. If I could write one called 16, we'd both be there, but I'm pretty sure that book would be banned immediately for underage sexcapades and extreme drug use. ;) #FuckingShannon. Jana asks me all the time how the hell I'm still alive when I wander down Memory Lane. Just lucky I got over that wild side early, I guess.

I changed everything about my family life except for where we lived, because honestly, you do not need to know about it. But it was dramatic enough to give me the idea for this book. And I'll tell you, the only good thing about my eighteenth birthday was Sunday.

He's real, but it didn't happen exactly the way I wrote it, and his name wasn't Danny, it was Geoff. I have two "love" regrets in life, and one of them was Geoff. I talked to him a few years ago on Facebook and that was pretty cool. He reminded me of the "J" he tattooed over his heart and I reminded him of how my 18th birthday really went down. :) And even though he really was a drug dealer, he was Sunday. His whole personality was Sunday. He is forever the guy who took care of me when I had that ear infection. Dr. Geoff, he said. "Just call me Dr. Geoff."

When he got his first apartment after we broke up he called me on the phone and said, "Come over. I got this place and no one to share it with." So he picked me up and I went over there. Just writing this makes me smile because we were sitting on the floor and he asks me if I want to see his AK's under his bed. He'd moved up in the drug world since we dated. I was all, "Nah. I don't think so." But then he smiled and said, "Wanna see my banana clip, Julie?" *#FuckingSunday*. We laughed and he did show me his guns.

I *oohed* and *ahhed* with him. I cannot even picture him the way people must see him today. I only see that smile, that night, sitting on the floor of his bedroom in his very first apartment. I only saw him once after that because we were heading in two totally different directions. He called me right after my daughter was born and came over to see us. And soon after that I left Orange Country and started a new life somewhere else.

Which leads me to the characters. I think pretty much everyone named in the book is a real character, but again, the story was told to keep everyone out of it. So Danny, you weren't Sunday, but you were still a great friend. Phil was not a big time dealer, he was a fav of mine too, but there was a guy who lived in the house at the end of the alley who smoked me out on occasion. He was a fond memory from my 18th birthday, and not for that reason. And a guy I knew did live across Broadway in that house I gave Mateo, but we never dated. Rocky was real and I described her the way she looked back then. Danny in the book was actually a guy called Mark (I left Geoff out of this story for reasons you can probably imagine), and we were acquaintances. He was the kid sitting next to me while I had a meltdown in the office in Chapter One, and he really did tell all his friends about me, so that's how I found my people that last semester. The arcade was an ice cream shop called Mr. Happy's and that owner was also a friend. I ate at that restaurant, that cop did live across the way in my apartments, and I dated a much older man and did lots of dirty things with him, but he was not my teacher for night school and I was not 18 (yet). Not even close. LOL.

I did go to five high schools and the only evidence that I graduated from Anaheim, and not the school I started senior year in San Diego, is the 1987 group photo of the senior class standing out on the front steps. I have a Van Halen shirt on.

I skated though school. I'm smart. I was born that way. Just like Rook in Tragic was born tall, skinny and pretty— I was born smart. But I skated through school because I could. It did me no favors being smart. People still assumed I was stupid and it took me a much longer time to learn the lesson that Shannon learned at the end of this book.

Everything of worth requires effort.

The Colony, as that section of Anaheim is called, was my hood. These people and a lot of this story were real. I wrote Eighteen in two and a half weeks between Anarchy Found and Rook and Ronin HEA (releasing December 16th) because the world was already there. The characters were already there. It was written before I wrote it because I lived it.

Which brings me to why I wrote it. I saw a blog post about a book blogger who said she was breaking up with the New Adult genre. She had a lot of valid points. Too much angst, too much drama, too much of everything. I don't think she could relate.

But I can relate to that drama. Eighteen was hard for me. It was probably one of the most difficult times in my life because I was adrift. My family was not cohesive. It didn't pull me together, it unraveled long before I was moved out to California the middle of my junior year. But the drama that had me changing schools in the middle of senior year was real and overwhelming.

This is why I started writing new adult books to begin with. Rook in Tragic was drifting too. And people have asked a few times about which of my female characters I relate to the most, and although there is a lot of Veronica in me, Rook is the closest.

So I wrote this book for people who relate to drama and angst. I write all my books for them. Every book is filled with outsiders and anti-heroes because my whole life I've been on the outside, and while all my friends were good (or I wouldn't be friends with them), it was never in the traditional sense. Don't get me wrong, I like it here on the outside. I could give a fuck what the world does. I live my life the way I live it because I don't mind the outside. I like the fringe. And I put every bit of it into my books. People like Rook because they relate to her struggle, they admire her strength, and they want her to find that HEA.

I think I've found my HEA in books, just like a lot of you.

When the New Adult genre was just getting started people went crazy for it. It has since died down, but Coming of Age stories will never die down. Coming of Age is something we can all relate to. A few years ago when I wrote Tragic people were even asking if the New Adult genre was necessary and I remember writing a blog post for my book blog, New Adult Addiction, explaining why I thought it was relevant. There is a little bit of this story in that post. The reason it's relevant is because not everyone wants the sweet story. Sure, people read fiction to escape reality, but not everyone wants the perfect Mary Sue character to be saved by the billionaire and the perfect ending with two point five kids.

People want a little reality in their story. They want angst and drama. They want to read about the risk they never took, the fear they never felt, and the victory when the characters get it right. Or maybe they did take that risk, they did feel that fear, and they did/did not make it right. Maybe they relate the way I relate and just want to know that it's normal. That other people experienced coming of age that way too. Either way, I write for those people. And if you don't like what I write, well, there are a billion other books out there. Have at it. I'm gonna keep doing my thing.

***

So what's next? A brand new genre, that's all. Have you ever wanted to fuck Batman? Or Ironman? Well, you're gonna get your chance to experience the sexy world of superhero romance in the next book called Anarchy Found. You think I'm kidding? ;) Nah. You know me better than that. Anarchy Found is the first standalone book in a series about Alpha Superheroes. No Spiderman here. No Superman here. We like the outsiders, remember? The anti-heroes. We like Batman and Ironman because they are sexy as fuck and they don't take any shit. We like them because they have money, and power, and fuck hot Batcaves where they (should) take their women. They are dark, they are scary, and they have been off the market for romance… until now.

So get ready. I have hot Super Alphas coming and you can check out the story on the special website. (Make sure to check out the About Me section, I have a ton of pics! Are you on there?) The pre-order will go live on November 29th here and the book will release on December 2nd.

After that is the Rook & Ronin HEA novella called, Happily Ever After: (A Day in the Life of the HEA), releasing December 16th for 99 cents. One more look at Ford, Spencer, and Ronin and a sneak peak of what's to come with Five and Rory. No preorder. Join my newsletter list (link below) to be notified of when it goes live.

***

If you follow me on my author page on Facebook or my Twitter account, you know I run a lot of contests. I give away a lot of signed books and prize packages. That's how I like to connect with *#fans*. So if you want to win some cool stuff, keep in touch! I love interacting with fans and answering any questions you have about the characters or the story.

I have a really great Street Team. The best, in fact. They are awesome and we are like a family in there. I'm not taking new members, we are closed. But I do run a fan group on Facebook called Shrike Bikes. They are in there all the time, as am I. So if you'd like to hang out with us, just click the link and ask to join the group. One of us will approve you as soon as we see the request.

If you want to be notified of upcoming books, sign-up forms for advanced release copies (ARC's), special pre-release teasers, or how to order a signed copy of this book, you can sign up for my newsletter here.

Thank you for reading, thank you for reviewing, and thank you for *Getting Me*.

I'll see you in the next book!

Julie

About the Author

JA Huss never wanted to be a writer and she still dreams of that elusive career as an astronaut. She originally went to school to become an equine veterinarian but soon figured out they keep horrible hours and decided to go to grad school instead. That Ph.D wasn't all it was cracked up to be (and she really sucked at the whole scientist thing), so she dropped out and got a M.S. in forensic toxicology just to get the whole thing over with as soon as possible.

After graduation she got a job with the state of Colorado as their one and only hog farm inspector and spent her days wandering the Eastern Plains shooting the shit with farmers.

After a few years of that, she got bored. And since she was a homeschool mom and actually does love science, she decided to write science textbooks and make online classes for other homeschool moms.

She wrote more than two hundred of those workbooks and was the number one publisher at the online homeschool store many times, but eventually she covered every science topic she could think of and ran out of shit to say.

So in 2012 she decided to write fiction instead. That year she released her first three books and started a career that would make her a New York Times bestseller and land her on the USA Today Bestseller's List eighteen times in the next three years.

Her books have sold millions of copies all over the world, the audio version of her semi-autobiographical book, Eighteen, was nominated for a Voice Arts Award and an Audie Award in 2016 and 2017 respectively, her audiobook, Mr. Perfect, was nominated for a Voice Arts Award in 2017, and her audiobook, Taking Turns, was nominated for an Audie Award in 2018.

Johnathan McClain is her first (and only) writing partner and even though they are worlds apart in just about every way imaginable, it works.

She lives on a ranch in Central Colorado with her family.